"**Y**ou look good in white." He leaned closer to her and whispered, "I like it when you let out your hair. I remember it all over my pillow. I can't get the image out of my head." She tried not to inhale his perfume, but she lost the battle. She shifted in her seat and glared at him. "Let's not talk to each other."

"What did you say?" He brought his lips closer to her ear, and she could feel the hot air from his breath, "I can't hear you."

Jill bit her lips. "Larry, please behave. I want to have a relaxing time out. I can do without you whispering in my ear."

He straightened up. "Interesting. Do I still unsettle you?"

"You know you do," Jill whispered, "and I don't want that in my life right now. Can we pretend as if we don't share a past? At least for this evening."

"I can do that." Larry nodded. "Well, I guess I'll have to reluctantly introduce myself again. Hello, my name is Lawrence Robert Nelson, but everybody around here calls me Larry."

He pushed out his hand for her to shake. Jill looked at it and frowned. "My name is Jillian Wimple. Everyone around here calls me Jill."

Larry chuckled. "I have heard the surname Wimple before. Are you associated with the bakery at Crimson Hills?"

NO MORE MRS. NICE GIRL

BRENDA BARRETT

ALSO BY BRENDA BARRETT

FULL CIRCLE
NEW BEGINNINGS
THE PREACHER AND THE PROSTITUTE
AFTER THE END
THE EMPTY HAMMOCK
THE PULL OF FREEDOM
REBOUND SERIES
THREE RIVERS SERIES
NEW SONG SERIES
BANCROFT SERIES
MAGNOLIA SISTERS SERIES
SCARLETT SERIES
WILEY BROTHERS SERIES
PRYCE SISTERS SERIES
THE JACKSONS SERIES

ABOUT THE AUTHOR

Brenda Barrett is an award-winning and bestselling author who has a passion for writing real Jamaican romances.

When she's not weaving words that transport readers to exotic locales, you can find her nurturing her green thumb in the garden or doting on her beloved cats.

With an infectious zest for life, this author brings a unique perspective to her writing that is both relatable and thought-provoking.

Don't be surprised if you find yourself lost in the pages of her latest work, as she seamlessly blends romance with some drama, mystery, and suspense, or even sci-fi, leaving readers wanting more.

You can connect with Brenda online at:
Brenalbar.com
Twitter.com/AuthorWriterBB
Facebook.com/AuthorBrendaBarrett

Prologue

"**Y**our year is up, Rodney Charming." Noel White announced from the door of the pastor's vestry. "Who will it be?"

"Huh?" Rodney dragged his eyes from the computer screen. He was reading about the sentencing of twelve accountants from his brother's old firm. One had gotten a ten year prison sentence for a first-degree felony charge. It was harsher than what he had thought would be meted out for a white-collar crime. His brother probably would have gotten ten years, too, if he were alive.

That would have been a hard pill to swallow for his sibling, who had been used to the finer things in life. Maybe it was for the best that they had met in that car accident in Canada. Roderick had lost his life, and Rodney had escaped with only a mild concussion.

"Don't tell me you forgot?" Noel scowled. "You can't forget stuff like this, Rodney. I have faithfully texted you at the start of every month, and you have ignored me."

"What are you talking about, Uncle Noel?" Rodney asked. "You text me birdwatch every month. I just assumed you were into birds."

"It's not bird watch!" Noel growled, "It's bride watch. Can't you read, son? You have two doctorates; how can you mix up bride watch with bird watch!"

"Why would I be bride watching?" Rodney asked, further confused.

"Good God! That accident that took your brother's life has surely messed with your memory. I have never seen anything like it; you forget the conversations and dates we made. I cannot get used to it."

Rodney sighed. "It's true my head got banged up a bit, and I forget things, but it's not as bad as you are making out."

"It's bad, Rodney," Noel sat down heavily in the seat across from him and sighed. "I am retired and nearing seventy-five, and I have a better memory than you do."

Rodney sighed. "Can you kindly remind me what bride watch is about?"

"I called in favors abroad, and I leaned on the elders here to accept you into their ranks, with the provision that you would get married within a year. Think back, Rodney; they wouldn't budge on hiring you if you were single. So I told them to give you a year. Is anything coming back to you?"

Rodney opened his mouth and then closed it. "No, I absolutely forgot."

"Do you recall why they fired you from being the head pastor of the university church?" Noel leaned forward. "Don't tell me you have conveniently forgotten that."

"Well, I haven't forgotten," Rodney mumbled.

"Just in case, let me give you a little refresher," Noel said stoutly. "You called me a year ago frantic that you were going to go to jail because you were in a sexual relationship with a girl under the age of consent."

Rodney winced. "Really, it was her word against mine."

"Someone caught you two in your office and recorded it on their phone."

"Ah yes, there was that." Rodney inhaled. "I forgot about that."

Noel glared at him. "When I arranged for you to come to Crimson Hills to cool off a little, I used all my clout with the church board to set you up here. Now it's time to fulfill your end of the bargain and get married before the year ends! I will not be made to look a fool, Rodney Charming."

Rodney gulped. "Can you please speak in softer tones? I don't know if the church secretary is off the premises yet."

"She is off. I just saw her drive out. Why was she working so late?" Noel asked, concerned. "She is a married woman, not a suitable candidate. I hope you are not fooling around with her."

"She was working on our annual thanksgiving service program," Rodney said faintly, "No, I am not having an affair with her. I am staying far away from women for the time being."

"But you can't do that," Noel frowned. "That is not a part of the deal. You promised me you would find a nice woman and start a family when you came here. But you have gotten too comfortable. Paul Hunt is gone to study, and you feel as if you have time. You don't have time, Rodney. They will get a local person in your place in a few days if you don't sober up."

Rodney leaned back in his chair. "I don't understand. I am sober, straitlaced, and minister-like. I have never encouraged even one of the women who sniff around me with anything more than a smile."

"That's the problem," Noel sniffed, "there is talk in some circles that you are gay."

"Me!" Rodney laughed, "I have been called many things but never that."

"I had the same reaction." Noel chuckled. "If only they knew what I know, they would stop that nonsense. You made your brother look like a saint where women were concerned. I could never understand it.

"You are the one with several degrees in ministry and what not, and yet you could never find a woman who was satisfactory enough. You ruined some beautiful women in your time. They flock to you like ants to sugar, and they all got their hearts broken.

"And to think your accountant brother was the opposite. He married young, was faithful to his wife, loved her to death, and had a stable relationship. I wonder what went wrong with you?"

"I have no idea." Rodney cleared his throat. "Roderick found his soul mate. It is a very rare thing. Finding a soul mate is not as simple as it sounds."

"If he wasn't a criminal, he would have been the better twin." Noel sighed. "My poor sister was unlucky with her sons. I am glad she is not around to see this."

"Now come on, Uncle Noel." Rodney protested. "First of all, Roderick was not a criminal. He thought he was helping clients at his accounting firm. He did as he was told by the partners, no questions asked. Then when he found out what was going on, he resigned."

"I can give him that." Noel grunted. "He saw the writing on the wall and ran. It still doesn't negate the fact that he would be facing real jail time if he were alive, just like you. Maybe you two would have been cellmates. The Charming Brothers, identical twin boys who took different paths in life, one a pastor and one an accountant, both ending up behind bars. You can't make this up."

Rodney sighed and ran his hand over his face. "In my defense, that girl falsified her documents, got into the college, and targeted me from day one. Someone must have put her up to it to get me into trouble. I doubt she was fifteen years and eleven months old. She must have been the hardest-looking fifteen-year-old in the world."

"I believe you." Noel mumbled. "That is why I am helping you out. But my help is limited now. You have two weeks to get married. I have a list in my pocket." He withdrew a piece of paper and pushed it across to Rodney.

Rodney took the list and looked at it in disbelief, Kim, Carmen, Hilda, Jill, and Farrah. All of them were perfectly fine women. The only problem was that he was not evenly remotely attracted to any of them.

He glanced at the photo of Lailah that was on his desk, Roderick's wife, the only woman he could foresee himself being with.

"I don't like any of the women on here," he passed back the list to his uncle. "Maybe with the exception of Jill Wimple. I do love her cooking and her pastries."

"Then marry her," Noel said solemnly.

"Marry her!" Rodney sputtered. "Are you out of your ever-loving mind? I am not even one percent attracted to Jill. And I have no clue how she feels about me other than the fact that I am always sampling her delicious food. How will I convince her to marry me in two weeks?"

"Use your charm." Noel guffawed. "Isn't that your surname? Your father sure knew how to use his. He got my levelheaded sister to leave her lawfully wedded husband out here and follow him to Canada just a week after meeting him."

Rodney sighed. "What will happen if I don't marry Jill?"

"You'll lose this job. If you try to work elsewhere, you'll probably get caught and deported to Canada to face charges."

Rodney gulped. The thought of prison gave him a fearful feeling in his gut. "I'll marry her in two weeks. She likes me, I can tell. I'll tell her that the Lord told me she is the one."

Noel nodded. "Make it a small private wedding. I'll smooth it over with the brethren. I know you don't want the attention on you. Invite one or two key people so that there is no talk."

Rodney nodded, staring at his uncle but not seeing him. How would he get Jill Wimple to agree to any of this? She was a sweet, unassuming woman who was passionate about baking and Bible study. She was easy to talk to and had a wry sense of humor. He liked Jill as a friend. She was one of the first people he had warmed to after fleeing ignominiously from Canada.

She was probably the only person that knew some things about his background. After a slice or two of her decadent chocolate cake, he was usually mellow enough to drop a few details about himself into the conversation.

Jill liked him. She stared at him with hopeless adoration. He couldn't break her heart; he had to find a way to marry her and not let her get attached to him. This situation he was in was only temporary, he hoped to resolve it soon, and Jill Wimple was not a part of his long-term plans.

How could he pull off a marriage of convenience to the nicest woman in Crimson Hills?

Chapter One

Jill was standing at the noticeboard and staring at it in a daze.

"Did you hear a word I said?" Mercedes asked beside her.

Jill looked over at Mercedes, who was dressed in a slim-fit black power suit and felt a little pang of envy. It was just the other day that Mercedes came to the bakery, her hair in two long ponytails and her face covered in zits. She was a far cry from that now. The ponytails were replaced by long straight hair, and the zits had disappeared to reveal a glowing complexion.

Larry Nelson's little sister had grown up. She looked like a young professional who meant business.

How old was she now, twenty-four? How had she managed to stay so slim and shapely? And when had she gotten that commanding air? Jill felt like saying yes, ma'am, though she was the older of the two.

"I heard you," Jill said, "but I don't think I can squeeze in a wedding cake for Shay and Jeremiah on top of the thirty cakes for your mother. So why don't you use one of Bunny's cakes? All of them are elaborate, white and gold creations that could rival any wedding cake."

"Because Shay wants a fruit cake, and we planned the wedding at the last minute," Mercedes said patiently. "It's just a simple three-tier wedding cake for them to cut, and we share up with her family in little cake boxes that will say Shay and Jeremiah and have the date."

"I am happy for them, and normally I wouldn't mind doing it, but have you seen my noticeboard? That's our schedule," Jill pointed to the crowded noticeboard. "We have cakes up to our necks in the next couple of days. I would have to work late tomorrow night and then…."

"Don't worry about it. I will help," Mercedes said. "I can do some mixing, fetching and carrying, whatever you want. I am certainly no baking professional, but whatever will help, I'll do it."

Jill looked at her skeptically. "Aren't you a fancy psychologist now? Why are you so invested in this?"

"Because I helped Shay to face her fear of marriage. She finally made up her mind to marry my brother, and I will move heaven and earth to get her what she wants at this time. She wants a fruit cake, and you are the best baker on this side of Jamaica. I couldn't get her a store-bought cake for their big moment. And I am sort of the wedding planner. Mom was the one who suggested that we use her birthday party for the wedding since it's already a lovely venue. Besides, all of our family and friends will be there anyway. So it's perfect.

"By the way, Jeremiah doesn't know it's going to happen, so please don't say a word. He is coming back in two days."

"I do love a good romance," Jill sighed. "Okay, I'll do it. I will have to work late tomorrow night, but I'll get it done."

"Thank you, Jill," Mercedes hugged her and inhaled before letting her go. "You smell so good, like freshly baked cinnamon rolls."

Jill chuckled. "Thanks, I guess."

"Somebody should bottle that scent," Mercedes said, "I would put it in a diffuser and inhale it and remember."

"What does it remind you of?" Jill asked.

"My childhood, very happy times with my siblings and mom and dad. My mom insisted we eat together as a family on the weekends. So for two mornings, we would get our breakfast catered by your grandmother. I remember the scent of the food when it was dropped off. I especially remember the warm cinnamon rolls. Larry and I would fight over the cream cheese frosted ones until mom decided to order more of those than the regular glazed ones. Good times."

Jill smiled. "I have a few cinnamon rolls left over. Do you want some?"

"Yes!" Mercedes nodded. "I thought I was out of luck because it was closing time and there was nothing in the cases outside."

"It was a busy day. Sometimes we do have a complete clear-out of the display case. But I was saving a couple rolls for supper," Jill said, "which I probably shouldn't be having at this time of night anyway."

She went into her office, which was looking untidier than she was comfortable with, grabbed the box with the six juicy-looking cinnamon rolls all nicely frosted with cream cheese. She handed it to Mercedes.

"Don't you want to share?" Mercedes asked.

"No," Jill sighed, "I am trying to diet. I shouldn't be going upstairs with these anyway. I had a stressful day, and this is how I deal with it. My smart scale said I am two hundred and sixty pounds. It then sent a report to my phone. Apparently, I am morbidly obese and at risk of diabetes, heart disease, high blood pressure, stroke, and a couple of other lifestyle diseases that I can't remember, and I need to see my doctor or nutritionist immediately."

"Oh Jill," Mercedes said sympathetically, "you have to do something about your weight. You can't go on like this."

"I know." Jill sighed. "I did ask Lee Wiley a couple of months ago to help me, but then Dacy got out of prison, and he got married, and his new job is demanding."

Mercedes nodded. "But did you really want the help? It seems as if you are making many excuses for not following up with Lee."

They walked to the front of the store, and Jill felt her heart racing just a little bit too much for that short distance.

"I do want the help," Jill said, "I can't lose one hundred and twenty pounds on my own. I have tried, believe me, I have tried. I have done every diet known to man. I heard that losing weight is eighty percent food and twenty percent exercise. So I tried keto, Atkins, raw food, vegan, vegetarian, and zone diets. I tried to fast; I only ate a certain color food at one time. You name it, I've done it."

Mercedes nodded sympathetically.

"I have also tried exercising, I used to walk up and down these hills, but I quit because I had no one to walk with. I even pray about it, asking God to miraculously shrink me down to size, but of course, that's unreasonable, actions have consequences, and I do love food, especially sugary food. I fail every single time. I am at my wit's end at this point."

"You just need some motivation to stay consistent," Mercedes said gently. "You have to find something to make you stay focused on losing the excess weight. What do you really want right now in your life? What do you aspire to?"

Jill stared at Mercedes. "I don't know. I wanted to get this bakery to be more successful than when my grandma had it. I have far surpassed her in that regard, chiefly because of the new businesses popping up around Crimson Hills."

Mercedes nodded. "What about personally?"

"I er…" Jill sighed, "this is embarrassing, but I want to get married and have children."

"Why is it embarrassing?" Mercedes asked.

"It's not the modern thing to admit. Besides, I am everybody's friend," Jill said, "no one is thinking about me romantically. Do you know how many times I have heard this exact phrase; you would be so pretty if you weren't so fat. At the rate my life is going, I may never have a romantic interest, get married, or have children. Crimson Hills is full of handsome eligible men who view me squarely as their fat friend. And sometimes, I am fine with that, but at other times I see thirty coming toward me, and I know I will be lonely for life. It's either that or I will have to settle with someone who probably will fat shame me until I can't take it anymore, or even worse, I could get stuck with the likes of Dalton at church. He loves fat women. The fatter, the better. He actually thinks I am slim."

"What about Larry?" Mercedes asked. "My brother is into you."

Jill sighed. "Larry and I…we…had a thing one summer."

"I know," Mercedes nodded.

Jill cleared her throat. "How? We had to see each other in secret. My grandma did not exactly approve of us having a relationship."

"My powers of perception are well-honed," Mercedes grinned, "and even seven years ago, I could see that my brother was a goner. You were his first love. I think you tied him up into knots."

"I loved him too," Jill said, "but he was too young for me to trust his feelings, and I rebelled at twenty-one. I never had a boyfriend, or a guy interested in me till Larry. I still lived with my grandmother, who treated me like I was twelve, and Larry treated me like I mattered. He went off to college, and I stayed back to take over the bakery when my grandmother left, end of story."

Jill closed her eyes. She could still see Larry's woebegone face in her mind's eye when she told him in no uncertain terms, Larry, you have to move on. We are not each other's type. When you go to college and meet other girls, you will know exactly what I am talking about.

She had known instinctively that when Larry went to college and was exposed to all the gorgeous girls, he would not have given her a moment's thought. She had only preempted the inevitable by making it easy for him to move on. Mercedes thought he was still interested in her, but she was wrong.

Larry probably remembered their secret romance and wanted to rekindle it. There was something about doing stuff in secret with the hint of the forbidden that was appealing to people. It had appealed to her. She had repeatedly considered giving in to the not-so-subtle cues that he wanted them to be an item again since he came back a year ago.

"I don't want to talk about that time," Jill said loudly to Mercedes.

"You don't have to," Mercedes said, "I can guess what happened. You thought he was too young for you and too much of a bad boy. He was going through a rebellious phase at eighteen, while he tried to find himself. You were the good girl, three years older, conservative, and insecure about her weight.

"You tried to keep him at arm's length, but he fell for you too and wanted something serious, but you broke it off when he went to school in the States.

"It's been a year, and now he is back, and you are struggling to keep him at bay. Partly because you have gotten fatter and are ashamed of it and partly because you are now a dedicated Christian and don't want to fall into temptation."

Jill opened her mouth, and no sound came out.

Mercedes laughed. "How accurate was I?"

"How did you do that?" Jill finally spluttered.

"Deductive reasoning. I know you and Larry. I made some assumptions, and your response told me I was right. I could pretend to read palms if I wasn't a psychotherapist." Mercedes chuckled. "If you want some advice, I think Larry is perfect for you, and you don't have to keep him at a distance anymore."

"He is not perfect for me." Jill shook her head. "He is the opposite of what I want in my life now. I want a god-fearing, pious, morally upstanding, conservative person. I have no room in my life for a maverick. I am getting too old for adventure."

Mercedes hooted with laughter. "Larry is a rebel, sure, and not cut from a conservative cloth, but character is what matters. At the end of the day, he is the person you can call on when you are in trouble, and if I have a moral dilemma, I can guarantee you that he will err on the side of good, any day, all day.

"When you think about it, Larry is more Christian than some of the people you go to church with. He is kinder than anyone I know; he is not the judgmental type, and he doesn't lie. He would rather tell the truth than spare your feelings. Who do you know like that?"

Jill winced. "No one. Larry does have his good side, but

Mercedes, he is not ready for marriage or babies like I am. A good time, yes. A lifetime commitment, no. And I wouldn't ask it of him. He is young. He is living his life. He doesn't want a committed Christian woman who breaks church benches when she sits on them or can't hold in the front seat of his new sports car, or who gets teased or stared at outside of the Crimson Hill bubble.

"People still look down their noses at fat people and think they are fair game to be criticized and ostracized."

"Ah, Jill," Mercedes shook her head, "here's my card."

She pulled a card from her bag. "We need to work on that self-esteem of yours and get you motivated to lose the weight."

Jill took the card. "You can do that; you can motivate me to lose weight?"

"I can certainly try," Mercedes said.

Rodney Charming walked into the store, sparing her from asking Mercedes more about her miraculous abilities. He was dressed in his regular semiformal outfit: a dress shirt without a tie and black pants. This was not a casual call.

He smiled at both of them. "Jill, Mercedes."

"Hey, Pastor," Mercedes greeted him. "Am I still down for that teen counseling session you have planned for Wednesday?

"Oh, definitely," Rodney nodded. "The young people said they appreciated the last one so much that they are inviting friends this time. Apparently, you are not as stuffy and boring as I am, and you tell it like it is."

"Bless their hearts." Mercedes laughed. "Well, I am on my way to an online counseling session. Jill, call me if you want help with that cake."

Jill nodded. "I will."

Mercedes left the bakery, and Jill inhaled and then exhaled

slowly. She always felt a pang of regret when she discussed Larry Nelson. When he left Crimson Hills seven years ago, it had taken her a full year to get over his leaving.

He had tried calling, and her grandmother had only been too happy to tell him to stop. He had written her, and she had dumped his letters, unopened. There had been no future for them then, and there would be no future now.

She focused on Pastor Charming, pushing her regret about Larry aside. She felt a small tingle of annoyance when she looked at the pastor's handsome face. He was probably coming to discuss something about the annual thanksgiving program. It was beginning to feel as if she was the only volunteer for that day.

She had a long list of things she had volunteered to do for the event and had taken on the lion's share of the catering.

She was always left holding the bag at church. It was beginning to feel like her life was one long volunteer service.

Her problem was she couldn't say no. She was too much into people-pleasing. She wondered what new request the pastor had.

And to think she had plans for tonight. She would go upstairs to her living quarters, have a long hot shower, and eat her half dozen cinnamon rolls, while she read one of her latest romance novels and live vicariously through the fictional characters.

Well, that plan was scrapped. She had given Mercedes all of her cinnamon rolls, and she probably would have a long discussion with Pastor Charming about the annual thanksgiving service instead of the shower.

He would harp on and on about it having to be the best thanksgiving service the church had ever seen because he wanted to make an impact on the congregation before Pastor Hunt came back from his studies and took over the reins as senior pastor again.

She would sit and listen attentively, watch the handsome lines of his face, and wonder how she could make him like her? How could she make him see that she was a woman and desirable?

And he would just smile at her, in that way of his, like she imagined one would smile at a favorite pet.

He always told her she was the nicest person he knew. In her imagination that was a bit like a pat on the head.

Honestly, she was getting tired of hearing that. For once, couldn't she be the sexiest or prettiest or hottest girl somebody knew?

"Jill," Rodney urged, "can we talk?"

"Sure." Jill blinked at him and focused. He was standing almost directly in front of her.

"You zoned out there for a while," he smiled. She didn't realize that he was so close. She could smell his cologne. She was a stickler for men's cologne. Larry's cologne had turned her on just by a whiff of it. She inhaled Pastor Charming's.

There was nothing, a leap of her heart or quickening of her blood but it smelled good.

Jill cleared her throat and tried to focus. "I was thinking."

Her brief irritation with him disappeared.

How could she be annoyed at Rodney Charming? He was the current star in her fantasies. She had been dreaming about him nonstop these last couple of weeks. He had been down on his knees, begging her to marry him. The dream was so vivid she was beginning to wonder what it could mean.

Surely Pastor Charming was not interested in her like that. He saw her like everyone else, a pleasant overweight woman who would go the extra mile for the less fortunate and the stray cats in her community. The only person who would say yes to anything going on at church.

Nobody saw her as a sexual being who had passions and feelings and yearned for companionship.

Well, no one else except Larry Nelson.

She wasn't going to think about Larry. He wasn't the right person for her.

They were unequally yoked. They were totally different, especially when it came to spiritual matters. He was also too young, twenty-five to her twenty-eight, and he was too magnetic. He made her forget her principles. He was too much of a temptation to have around.

If her grandmother had not set her straight seven years ago, she would have lost her mind over Larry. He had been a teenager, just testing his powers over the female sex. She had gone far enough with him as it was.

On the other hand, Rodney Charming was exactly who she needed in her life. Not only was he comparable to Larry in the looks department, but he had all the attributes of what she wanted in a man.

Her grandmother had always said she would marry a man of God. And Rodney Charming was the one. Her heart did little palpitations when he spoke, especially when he preached.

He had a smooth and husky voice, and he looked quite a bit like Shemar Moore. When he had just come into the district, they couldn't believe that he would be in their church district and not acting in some production with Crimson Hill as a backdrop.

He was tall, with medium-toned brown skin, which looked golden when he was in the sunlight. He had impossibly white even teeth and a smile that could probably melt chocolate. His eyes were a light brown, almost like honey.

"I was hoping we could sit down," Rodney said hesitantly.

"I anticipate that this will take a while."

"Well, I was about to lock up and go upstairs." Jill said. "I badly need a shower and to unwind from today. One of my cashiers had an emergency at home, and I had to fill in for her and do some last-minute deliveries."

"I'll join you upstairs," Rodney said. "What I have to say to you is somewhat urgent and personal in nature."

Chapter Two

Jill looked at Rodney Charming in shock. He had never come up to her apartment before. What could be so urgent and personal that he needed to be in her private space? Not that she was complaining, this was a dream come true.

Her heart pounded in anxiety, and she wiped her hand on her black slacks. Maybe this was what her dream was about.

Maybe he would tell her that he was getting married and wanted her to bake him a wedding cake or tell her about his deep-abiding love for some woman at church. People always confided in her.

He was no different. He had told her about his identical twin brother and how much he had loved and still missed him after the car accident.

She was everybody's big comforting confidant, who would smilingly ply them with pastry and listen to their woes.

Suddenly she hated herself. She didn't want to hear Pastor Charming's confessions about someone else.

She wanted to be pinned by that honeyed gaze with undying love shining from his orbs.

She sighed. She was reading too many romance books, and she had leftover envy from all the pairings going on around her at Crimson Hill. Literally, all her friends were married now or preparing to get married. Romance was in the air, and she wanted some of it to come her way.

She was ripe for it.

"Okay," she said out loud. "I usually walk at the side entrance and spend some time with the cats when I go up, but since your car is still in the parking lot, you can come this way."

He followed her around the display cases and into the kitchen.

"Wow, it's huge," he said, looking around. "I didn't know it was so grand around here."

Jill smiled proudly. "For years my grandmother worked at a commercial bakery in Kingston before she came to Crimson Hill. She tried to replicate her old workplace here. She didn't get the memo that this is in the country, and she would have a smaller clientele. I am happy she built it like this. We have room to grow the business and have been steadily expanding. I love it."

"Ah," Rodney murmured. "Your grandmother, the infamous Sally Wimple, I am so sorry that I did not have the pleasure of meeting her. She is spoken of so highly by the eldership to this day. Is that her picture?"

He pointed to a picture of Sally in her apron, holding up a long loaf of bread. It was prominently situated beside the notice board in the Wimple Bakery gallery of pictures. It was crowded with pictures of their greatest cake masterpieces.

Jill nodded. "That's her."

"Where is she now?" He asked.

"She decided to travel so she left the bakery to me," Jill said, "her children and grandchildren are scattered all over the world. She wanted to spend a year with each of them. She has been gone for five years. At this rate, she'll probably return here in fifteen years. There are many of us in the Wimple clan, with one being born yearly."

"So, where is the picture of you?" Rodney asked, leaning closer to the board.

"I don't really like taking pictures," Jill grimaced, "I prefer taking pictures of the cakes."

He looked at her and smiled. "You are so modest and humble. A pretty girl like you should be taking pictures and plastering them everywhere."

Jill blushed; she turned her head away from his whisky-colored brown eyes. They seemed so intense. He called her a pretty girl. Now, that was a first for him. He had never complimented her before.

"Do you want a tour?" she hurriedly changed the subject. She had never been able to accept compliments with grace. Mostly because she didn't believe them.

"Sure," he nodded.

"Well, the offices are through here." She walked into the passageway, which was off the food prep area. That's my office, Grandma's old office, and Cambria's office. She is the head pastry chef. God sent her to this place when I was really swamped. She has been a blessing."

Rodney nodded. "I heard her story; it was quite miraculous."

"Crimson Hill is a place of miracles." Jill walked back out into the prep area. "I walk through here," she pointed to a back door and opened it into another passageway, "and then I head upstairs to the living quarters."

She climbed a flight of stairs, punched in her alarm code,

opened the door, and turned on the lights. "Welcome to my home."

"It is lovely. I am impressed." He walked over to the large sliding doors that opened to a modest patio area and looked outside. "The open plan design makes the place feel quite airy."

Jill smiled.

The place had two large bedrooms and bathrooms, a large kitchen, and an open-plan living room. Her grandmother had ended up with what could only be described as a cozy bohemian décor with lots of bright jeweled colors, which brightened up the brown wood furniture and light grey walls.

"Thank you, Pastor Charming," Jill said, "have you had supper? I could make some sandwiches."

"I already ate, thanks." He sighed. "Jill, could you call me Rodney, please. Pastor Charming seems a bit formal."

Jill smiled. "Well, Rodney, it is. Since you are not hungry, would you mind terribly if I take a shower? Grimy does not begin to describe how I feel."

"Sure," He nodded. "I'll just sit here and wait till you get back."

Jill nodded jerkily and headed to her bedroom. She had long since taken over the master suite as her own and remodeled it to her taste. She was more of a minimalist than her grandmother was. Though she appreciated the colors and warm tones of the rest of the house, she preferred all white and grey tones for her sleeping area. Something about the lack of color was restful for her.

She looked in her closet anxiously. What was she going to change into after her shower? It had to look casual, as if she wore it every day and not just to impress Pastor Charming… no, Rodney.

He said to call him Rodney.

She grinned and flitted through her maxi dresses. Most of them were flattering to her ever-increasing size, and they did look casual without making her appear as if she was trying too hard.

She pulled out a blue one with long bell sleeves that hid her arms. Her arms were her worst feature, always had been. They were big and round with an ever-increasing flap of flesh, making even her four xl tops harder to fit in these days.

She took off her clothes and looked at herself critically. There were no two ways about it. She was pear-shaped with more weight below her waist. Her big, thunder thighs and hanging belly were quite a sight when she was naked.

But she was tired of being critical of herself.

She had been her worst critic for the past sixteen of her twenty-eight years on the planet. She had come to accept that maybe she would always be obese. It was too hard to change, and she was never going to be motivated to lose the weight.

She ran a bakery, loved food, and being slim was not her future.

At least her face wasn't that bad, though her double chin was becoming more pronounced lately.

Facially she wasn't bad looking at all, even when she used to be teased in prep school; one of her little tormentors had told her that she was pretty for a fat girl.

She had almond-shaped eyes, a pert nose, and full pouty lips. Her nutmeg-brown complexion was smooth and blemish-free for the most part. It took many slices of cake for her to have an uninvited zit or two.

And Rodney had called her pretty. The question was, what was he buttering her up for?

The thought nagged her through her shower and even

when she put on her clothes.

She even put in hoop earrings and light makeup and let out her hair. She couldn't remember if he had ever seen her with her hair out. It was convenient for her to keep it in a bun at work and even at church. She usually helped to serve at their weekly potlucks.

Her hair helped her to feel slimmer. It was long, curly, and big and hit her somewhere around where she imagined her waist should be. When she fluffed it out, people forgot that she was fat. They stared at her hair instead.

Why was she making the extra effort? When he would probably be talking to her about his love for another woman? Just in case she was wrong, she gave her curls an extra fluff and stepped out into the hall, a trail of perfume following her as she approached him.

He was listening to her motivation to lose weight CD. She had bought it on a whim last week after her doctor had given her a rundown of all the diseases she was exposed to by being obese.

She inwardly cringed.

He would know that she had insecurities about her weight. She didn't want that. She liked to pretend that she was quite fine with how she was. She verbally preached body positivity and being satisfied with where she was weight-wise, but inside she envied everyone who wasn't overweight. They didn't have to be slim, just not as big as she was.

"Hey, wow, you look nice!" he looked up at her appreciatively.

"Thank you," Jill sat down across from him. That was her aim, and he did say wow, didn't he?

"And you smell great too. Black opium, isn't it?" He inhaled the air.

"Yes," Jill relaxed on the settee.

"At least I remember something. The accident really did a number on me." He cleared his throat. "I hope you don't mind; I was just checking to see if you had any good music, and this was in the player."

"I don't mind," Jill tensed up, "I try to listen to it in the morning before I go to work. I want to lose weight. My doctor says I need to lose one hundred pounds to be in the healthy normal range for my height, but I am just not motivated. I am not consistent."

"I think I understand," Rodney nodded. "I also struggle with finding consistency in some aspects of my life. I will power through and do the work if I have something to look forward to at the end."

"I know that in theory," Jill said. "I think I have a mental block when it comes to practice."

"Not in all aspects of your life, though." Rodney looked at her admiringly. "You really got this bakery off the ground, didn't you? You made it bigger than when your grandmother had it. At least, that's what everyone says."

Jill nodded. "It is true that I made a go of it when she left. I worked myself into the ground and was the only one doing all the baking."

Rodney nodded. "So, what made you so motivated to do that?"

"I wanted to prove to my parents that I could make a go of things." Jill sighed, "all of my family are academically inclined. I am not. My parents have two doctorate degrees, and both my brothers have PhDs. I have something to prove in my little corner of the world."

"I see," Rodney smiled. "And were they impressed?"

"Not quite." Jill sighed. "The other day my mother congratulated me on not letting the business tank. My father said at least I was keeping busy. The only thing that would make those two happy is if I got a doctorate or married a man with one."

Rodney frowned. "Oh really?"

"Unfortunately." Jill nodded, "they are the way they are, and I am the way I am."

"I see," Rodney murmured, "so pleasing your parents would motivate you to lose weight too?"

"Not really." Jill shrugged. "My parents are not troubled much by my weight. My lack of degrees and my lack of suitable prospective mates is more troublesome to them. In fact, my brothers have made it harder for me. They both got married to suitable women with PhD's as well. So the spotlight is on me now."

"So what would motivate you to lose the weight then?" Rodney asked. "What do you want, Jill?"

Jill licked her lips nervously. This was the second time in one day that somebody was asking her the same question. And while she could tell Mercedes about marriage and children, she couldn't tell him that. She was not about to confess her innermost desires to Rodney Charming.

"You are putting me on the spot," she said huskily. "I made a vow to not lie after a prayer and fasting session last year. Not even little white ones. I am having the most difficulty adhering to it now, but because you asked, I want marriage and children."

He smiled. A slow smile that had her watching the curve of his lips as it slowly grew wider and wider.

"You know you are the perfect woman for what I am about to ask. It feels like this is divinely ordained."

"Oh," Jill's voice was husky. "If it has to do with God, I am for it."

"I know." Rodney nodded. "That's what I like about you. You are one of the few genuine Christian women I know. And that's saying a lot. I used to work at a Christian university. Maybe we can help each other."

"How?" Jill asked. To say she was intrigued would not begin to describe her. She was eager to help Rodney Charming with whatever he wanted help with.

"You see," he was focused on her intently, his expression enigmatic. "I am just going to lay my cards on the table. I need a wife."

"Huh?" Jill could swear he just said he needed a wife. Maybe he said you need to get a life.

"I know this sounds like it is coming from left field. You and I have not really talked in that way. We only see each other at church or when I come here to get pastries, but I promise you, this is not a joke."

"It's not a joke?" Jill barely squeaked out.

"No," Rodney shook his head. I made a deal with the church leadership a year ago that I would be married in a year. As you can see, it hasn't happened yet, and the year is almost up. I need to be married in two weeks. Will you marry me?"

"Me?" Jill's mouth could barely function.

"Yes, you." Rodney said eagerly, "there was a list of women. You were the one that I could foresee marrying. So before you protest, hear me out."

Jill nodded eagerly as if she would ever protest. This was her dream come true, well he wasn't down on one knee, but he was asking her to marry him, just like in the dream!

"We could get to know each other after the marriage vows. There will be no intimacy expected. We could consummate the marriage after you lose a hundred pounds. That would give us time to get to know each other, and it could motivate you to lose the weight, I hope."

Jill wanted to shout yes, a thousand times yes, but

something held her back. She probably wouldn't lose a hundred pounds in the next ten years. She might never lose weight. And where would that leave her? Married with no sex, that's what.

"Jill?" Rodney asked tentatively. "The silence is giving me a complex. I thought you liked me, even a little."

"I do like you," Jill said, "I just can't remember being at one sixty pounds. I haven't seen that number on the scale since I was twelve. And if I never reach there, then what?"

"You will reach there," Charming said soothingly, "you want marriage and children, remember? This is motivation."

Jill nodded. She did. But with him? Somehow the thought didn't feel perfectly right.

"I need to keep my job here for the time being, and I am on the verge of losing it if I don't get married." Rodney urged.

"But that's archaic. Do you want me to talk to the elders on the board? Surely, they can't uphold such a mad idea."

"Oh no," Rodney shook his head. "I would rather we don't tell anyone unless it is absolutely necessary. We have to keep up appearances and act like a normal couple in public."

"I am not good at acting," Jill said ruefully. "And I would have to tell my friends. Keeping this kind of secret would make me spontaneously combust. I would stress myself out over it and then eat my weight in sugar to handle the stress."

"You know yourself well," Rodney murmured.

"Quite well." Jill said, "I did not get this big by accident."

"The fewer people involved, the better." Rodney cleared his throat. "Maybe you should tell them that we will have a super-secret wedding, and then we'll have a bigger one when you lose the weight."

Jill frowned. "I know them. They won't like it. They'll think this idea is ridiculous. Besides, they all know I will do a traditional wedding if I ever get married. I want all the frills and fuss."

"I bet they'll be very understanding and happy for you when they hear that at the end of this, you'll be getting a man with two PhDs and a proper marriage and children. Your parents will be pleased." Rodney urged. The desperation was spilling over in his voice.

"Oh, they will be pleased," Jill imagined her mother's delight at hearing that she was marrying a man with two PhDs, and a warm feeling overtook her.

She would finally be worthy. Well, half worthy. Her mother would prefer if she was the one getting the two PhDs, but a husband with two would surely be enough get her mother off her case.

But she wasn't going to tell them a word until it was a proper marriage, and they could have a big wedding.

Her family on both sides would not entertain a private marriage. They wouldn't understand an arrangement like this with Rodney. She couldn't even tell her grandmother either. She could do without the questions and the grief such an arrangement would bring.

"So, erm… where would we live anyway?" Jill asked, "I don't want to live at the manse."

"We don't have to live together for now," Rodney said earnestly. "You can live here. I'll live at the manse, and then we can have dinner a couple of times per week and get to know each other better. We'll revisit this original agreement when you lose that hundred pounds."

"I don't know." Jill bit her lip, "it sounds good, but it feels a little like lying."

"Lying to who?" Rodney asked. "How we pursue this, Jill, is nobody's business but ours. As I said, the details can be kept secret."

"I'll think about it," Jill said slowly.

"Thank you for thinking about it," Rodney said feelingly. "But please remember I don't have much time."

Chapter Three

"**I** may be getting married in two weeks!" Jill said to her captive audience of four. The store was closed for the day. She had asked them to come for a special meeting at seven.

They were her closest friends and deserved to hear the truth about her situation. The marriage details were not something she could keep to herself.

As it was, she had tossed and turned since Rodney's proposition, and she hadn't had a moment's peace in her head.

She had served freshly made pizza to her friends and had waited until they were digging into their lava cake which she had baked especially for them, before she made her announcement.

Dacy almost choked on her slice of cake.

Lee stopped chewing and looked at her, stunned. Cambria swallowed quickly and started laughing. Jack laughed with her.

"It's not funny, guys," Jill said. "If I go through with this, I'll be getting married in a couple of days. It's a private wedding, just me, Pastor Charming, two witnesses, his uncle, Noel, and his wife, Jane. I haven't told a soul about this yet, only you guys. I am even keeping it quiet from my family for now."

"Hold up," Dacy was the first to speak. "You may be marrying a man with whom you are not on a first-name basis?"

"Yikes," Jill grinned, "he told me I could call him Rodney. I am just so used to calling him Pastor Charming."

"Good heavens, it's not a joke," Jack said hoarsely. "Why would you marry this guy? And do it in secret, no less?"

"I just don't understand," Lee said, confused. "Cambria said he was not interested in you, just your pastries."

Dacy poked him in the side.

Lee straightened up. "That's a secret?"

"No, it's not," Cambria finally spoke. "He comes in here all the time, and Jill makes a big fuss over feeding him and refuses to let him pay. He smiles at her, and she walks around floating on cloud nine because of that user."

"If they are going to get married," Jack said, "maybe they were getting up to things behind the scenes."

"No, we are not," Jill said. "I was totally surprised when he asked me last night. He says he agreed to get married within a year when he came here, and now the year is almost up."

"Why would he agree to get married in a year?" Dacy asked skeptically. "What was he up to before, and why would that be a clause?"

"We don't usually hire single pastors," Jill said, "not since we had an incident with erm…Pastor Green."

"You mean the pastor that was caught in a compromising

position with the boy from the orphanage?" Jack asked. "Or was he the one who was caught in the car with his niece at the side of the road in the early morning hours by the police?"

Jill winced. "Pastor Green was the one caught with the boy, and Pastor Lewis was caught with the niece. Both were single and embarrassed the church because of that. The board has a no-tolerance clause for single pastors. They have to either be married or engaged before they are hired."

"I see," Dacy nodded. "I think it is unfair to the single pastors because who is to say that the married ones are any better?"

"Honey," Lee touched Dacy's hand, "let's not go off on a tangent here. Jill is getting married to her pastor so he can keep his job. That's the issue."

"Oh right," Dacy grimaced, "Jill is getting married. Pinch me."

"No," Lee kissed her on the lips instead.

"Come on, you two," Jill said, "haven't you gotten over the honeymoon stage yet?"

"No," Lee said, "we've been married for just eight months, give us another couple of years."

"I can't wait for our honeymoon," Jack smiled at Cambria, "four months has never seemed so long."

Jill sighed. It was par for the course when she was hanging out with newlyweds and people who were so hotly in love they couldn't see straight. Crimson Hill was filled with love these days.

Lee and Cambria's parents Chevelle and Othneil Wiley, had invited her to their small backyard wedding, surrounded by family and friends. Jill had cried throughout their heartfelt vows. She was a sucker for that kind of thing. Chevelle and Othneil were people who had found their way back to each other despite the odds.

Even Lee and Dacy had their own heartfelt story. She had cried at their wedding too. Dacy had been in prison for five years, and Lee had waited for her. They had married in an impromptu ceremony a few weeks after Dacy was released from prison.

And Cambria had come to Crimson Hills to find Jack when he lost his memory and forgot her and, in the process, had found her family. Jack had fallen in love with her all over again. And now they were getting married in sixteen weeks.

Her story with Pastor Charming was falling flat.

It wasn't romantic. It lacked sizzle. She was basically marrying the man because he wanted to keep his job. They would only consummate the marriage when she lost a hundred pounds. It surely didn't sound like any romantic story she had ever heard.

"We won't have a honeymoon until I lose a hundred pounds," Jill said out loud. "Actually, the marriage, along with helping him, is also for me to be motivated to lose weight."

"What on earth?" Dacy gasped, "No sex till you lose weight?"

"No." Jill shook her head, "and I am fine with that. I wasn't at first, but the truth is we really don't know each other that well. I would prefer to get to know him while I lose weight. Who knows, love may blossom in that time, and I will have a love story like you guys."

Her friends looked at each other in silence.

"It sounds like you are settling," Jack said, "suppose after this weight loss period, you don't like him at all. I think this guy is using you. I don't believe you are getting the better end of this bargain."

"And what if you don't lose a hundred pounds?" Cambria asked.

"I guess we can renegotiate," Jill said, looking down at her nails.

"Is there a renegotiate clause in this contract?" Cambria asked, "you'll be tying up her life with the pastor for who knows how many years."

"There is no contract," Jill said faintly, "we verbally agreed that when I lose the weight, we'd have a big wedding. I need the motivation to lose the weight."

"And you will lose it," Lee said determinedly, "Cambria is assuming that you won't lose the hundred pounds. I can help you. We can work on a meal and exercise plan. I've helped several women lose over a hundred pounds in less than a year. Weight loss is not that hard to do when you get a few key things right and decide to do them and change some habits."

Cambria nodded. "That's all good and well, but I have seen Jill when she is stressed. She is known to consume dozens of donuts in the space of an hour or a whole frosted double-layer sheet cake in a day."

"I only did that once," Jill protested. "I couldn't sell it to anyone, and I didn't want to waste it."

Cambria shook her head. "I have seen you with the donuts and the cinnamon rolls, not to mention the chocolate-filled croissants. Your powers of resistance are next to nil."

"I will help her," Lee said, "that's what I do."

"How will you fit Jill in when we'll be in St Lucia for six months?" Dacy asked.

"St Lucia?" Jill asked, "why?"

"Golden Acres has taken over another retirement resort there," Lee said. "The owners, Ace and Quade, asked me to go and set up the fitness department, train some people, and make sure it is running as it should."

"And I am going because I don't want to be away from him, not even a day," Dacy said dreamily.

"I understand that," Jill murmured, "but who is going to make sure I stay on track, and how will I handle this weight loss business without Lee?"

"I'll help you," Larry said behind them.

Everybody snapped their heads around.

"When did you get in here?" Jill gasped, "and how much of this did you hear?"

"The door was open, and I walked in," Larry said, "you guys were so caught up in your discussion you didn't hear when I quietly came in and sat down. I initially thought about making my presence known, but the conversation got too juicy."

"Argh, you are so frustrating," Jill growled, "I don't want you to know my business. Why are you even here?"

"I saw the light on at the end of the store. I wanted to see who you were entertaining."

"Are you stalking me now?" Jill sniped, "what does it matter who I was entertaining?"

"I am not stalking you," Larry grinned, "I walk by this place at night. When I have the time. Walking is therapeutic, and the hills are punishing. After I walk, I do a weight training session at my home gym."

"I set up his home gym," Lee said proudly, "it is state of the art."

"I can make sure you walk every night, and then you can train with me," Larry said. "I can be your accountable buddy."

"No thanks," Jill said grumpily. "I will have to find another personal trainer if Lee is unavailable. Besides, Cambria has a home gym. Her parents work out, and Jack works out."

Jack cleared his throat. "I am not consistent. I need to find time to plug it into my schedule. Besides, running the farm is not a walk in the park. I wish I could bulk up like Larry. I remember when Larry was skinny like me. Now he looks like a fitness model."

"He does." Dacy grinned. "I couldn't believe it when I saw you again. I was like, Larry Nelson is working out. He could give Lee Wiley, the love of my life, serious eye candy competition."

Larry laughed and flexed his biceps. "Thanks, Dacy."

Lee chuckled. "He isn't looking shabby. In fact, he was a male model when he was in college. I saw a fitness magazine with him on the front, and I was like, hold on a minute, that's Larry Nelson, the rebel of Crimson Hills."

"It was easy money." Larry grinned. "And there was this girl who kept insisting that I do it."

Jill glared at him. "It would have to be a girl, wouldn't it?"

She turned to Cambria before Larry could respond. "What about your parents? Can't I work out with them?"

"You don't want to be around them," Cambria chuckled, "they lock the gym door when they are 'working' out. I heard Othneil telling Chevelle that clothing was optional."

"Goodness," Jill murmured. "You are right, now is not the time to be the third wheel to honeymooners."

Lee laughed. "I am so happy I am not there with them when they are living their second chance at a life together."

Jill looked back at Larry furtively, and he caught her.

He winked.

She dragged her eyes away from his quickly. She had never mastered the art of staring Larry in the face. If she stared at him too long, her body started to tingle. She had no idea why he still affected her that way. She should have been immune to him by now.

"What about the lady at your gym who helped Jack with his physiotherapy?" She had to choke out the question. The Larry effect was taking her over. Her body was never comfortable and settled when he was near.

"Tenaj?" Lee raised an eyebrow. "She is booked and busy, both at Golden Acres and with private clients. She is working with Jack's father now, isn't she?"

Jack nodded. "And she is doing a good job, he is making strides, moving his arms more, and his speech is a little clearer."

"Jill, it may be best that you take Larry up on his offer to help," Dacy said, looking between her and Larry. "That is if you really want to lose weight to have your, er, honeymoon with Pastor Charming."

Larry winced. "I don't like that Charming guy, and I hate that you are thinking of marrying him."

"No one here is fond of him either, and we don't endorse this so-called marriage." Dacy said and then glanced at Jill. "Sorry."

Jill sighed. "I think he is lovely, an answer to prayers. If God says he is the one, he is the one."

Larry snorted. "Jill, your naivete is astounding. You should investigate that man's background and explore your compatibility before marrying him. You are assuming that because he is a pastor and has two doctorates, he is some kind of saint. Why is it that he is here in Crimson Hills at this time? And why does he need to keep his job so badly that he is marrying you? What or who is he hiding from?"

"I don't know," Jill glared at him, "but he is a good man."

"And you know this how?" Larry asked.

"I feel it," Jill said. "I am not as cynical as you are. Something does not always have to be happening behind the scenes. You are paranoid."

"Maybe I am," Larry said, "but something is not right with this guy, and I am not going to sit back and watch you make a fool of yourself over him."

Their audience was transfixed, looking between the two of them with undisguised interest.

"Stop talking!" Jill growled.

"Okay, I'll stop talking," Larry shrugged, "but if I were you, I would ask some basic questions before you tie yourself to him. Goodnight, all."

He got up and walked out, closing the door behind him.

"Amen," Dacy murmured in the silence that he left behind.

Cambria and Jack nodded in unison.

"I totally agree with what he said," Lee murmured. "You should check out this guy."

Jill glared at them, "I can't believe you are taking Larry's side! There is nothing wrong with Pastor Charming. He has had an abiding hate for the man from the moment he arrived here in Crimson Hills. Larry doesn't like pastors, even the good ones. For some reason, they upset his equilibrium."

"I can understand why he is like that?" Jack grinned, "wasn't he supplying one of your pastors with marijuana at one time?"

Jill sighed. "Yes, he was. Pastor Richards was weak and a bad witness. Larry deliberately led him astray."

Jack chuckled. "Larry was a kid; he has always been unfairly judged for your pastor's actions. Imagine blaming a teenager for your drug habit and taking zero responsibility for your own actions. And when you are caught blaming it on the teenager, and the congregation goes along with you. Madness."

"I didn't go along with Pastor Richards," Jill said waspishly, "I had better sense than that."

Jack shrugged. "The point is, Larry would be a hundred

times suited to you than the pastor. I don't know why you are fighting your attraction to him. You can't be in the same room without sparks flying."

Dacy and Lee were nodding vigorously.

"It's as if you light up," Dacy said. "I wouldn't be marrying one man while feeling that way about another. That's a recipe for disaster."

Jill pondered that statement as she saw them off one by one and then locked the store. They had shaken her confidence that she was doing the right thing. But she was going to go through with it. This may be her only chance at romance, and she would embrace it with open arms. Good and unexpected things did not just fall into her lap like this every day, and she had gone through some really dark days.

She turned off the lights and headed to her living quarters while she remembered how it was.

Chapter Four

"Jillian Wimple, are you eating again?" Her mother asked sharply. "Haven't you been taking the appetite suppressing pills I had the labs formulate just for you?"

"I take them, but they are not working." Jill looked up guiltily from the fridge door. Her mouth bore the remains of the frosting from her mother's birthday cake which tasted so good because her grandmother, Sally Wimple, baked it.

Every bite had made her feel better about herself. The teasing at school had been terrible today. Her parents had urged her to join one of the after-school clubs, and she had reluctantly done so. She wouldn't have bothered if she had known that they would use her as a laughingstock today.

"Good Lord, what are we going to do with you?" Zara Wimple looked horrified. She took in Jill's red eyes and the cake in her hands and on her mouth.

"Jill, you have got to stop stress eating. You are not doing yourself any favors."

"They used me as their before." Jill choked. She slammed the refrigerator door and walked toward the breakfast nook with her plate piled high with cake.

"What are you talking about?" Zara asked.

"It's health week. They had a lecture at my club. They had me stand up on stage as the before and had Piper Miller stand up as the after." Jill sniffed, "every time the speaker spoke about bad habits and the million and one things that happen to fat people, he pointed to me. And he pointed to Piper every time he spoke about the good things. Everybody laughed and made a moo sound when he pointed at me. When he pointed to Piper, there were cat calls, whistles, and cheers."

"Oh no," Zara looked at her daughter sympathetically. "Jill, I am so sorry. I know people can be cruel and awful, but at the end of the day, you must realize that your self-worth should not be tied up in your size or appearance. It should be tied to your brain. What's up here."

"That's the point, Mom. I am dumb, and I am fat. People hate me because of that. I don't fit in anywhere. I wish I was never born."

"Then what would your dad and I do. We love you, my precious only girl." Zara hugged her around the neck. "And you are not dumb. I am going to talk to the school about this. This is one humiliation too far."

"You don't need to bother." Jill grunted, "you can't stop people from being mean, and I volunteered for it. I raised my hand and volunteered to be the before."

"You can't help yourself, can you?" Zara sighed, "I told your father that you needed therapy for this, and he said we shouldn't try to cure you of being nice. He doesn't get that you have a need to be nice; people-pleasing, especially when it will lead to your own humiliation, is not good. I don't have to be a psychologist to figure that out. As for that school, we pay an arm and a leg to send you there. I can stop them from making your life a living hell. They will learn to stop picking on Zara Wimples' daughter."

"Maybe it wouldn't be so bad at public school. The children would be more normal there," Jill said, "at private school, the girls are snotty, and the boys are rude. Thank God today is my last day before the summer holidays."

"But that school is the best," Zara said earnestly. "Sending you there will put you on the fast track to university. That's where your brothers went. They both graduated at sixteen and were on their way to terminal degrees in their early twenties. That's what we want for you, too, Jill. We couldn't provide less than the best for you."

Jill sighed. She couldn't compare to her genius brothers, and she had no idea why her mother was blind to that. Her mother was deluded into thinking she had the smarts to be an astrophysicist like Ryan or a geologist like Zain. Both of them were on to their doctorates, and they hadn't even hit twenty-five.

"I was hoping you would take after your dad and me and become a mathematician. Her mother said dreamily, and then we could all work at the same university together, Drs. Zara, Phillip, and Jillian Wimple. In the same faculty."

Jill winced. She couldn't think of a more boring existence. She would much rather be in a kitchen baking something.

She wanted to be a baker like her grandmother, Sally. Her father's mother could combine the most mundane-looking ingredients into something awe-inspiring.

She scooped a mound of cake in her mouth and chewed deliberately. It sucked being a thirteen-year-old girl to parents who were overachievers. They couldn't see that she was not like them.

They had two brilliant boys, and they assumed their combined DNA would produce another brilliant child when she came along. Instead, they got her, and no amount of pretending wasn't going to fix her into being like them.

She wanted to be like them, though, because she knew her mother would be happy, but pretending to like mathematics or the sciences for the rest of her life was stressing her out.

The more stressed out she was, the more she ate. Why couldn't she just be…normal? The stress of trying to be perfect for her parents was not doing her any favors.

She looked at her mother with her perfectly made-up face and her slim, almost too-thin frame and wondered why she was so different from her.

Zara was a South African woman whose father still lived in South Africa. He was a world-renowned engineer. Zara's mother remarried and moved to Jamaica when she was young. She was a scientific researcher until her death. She died before Jill was born.

Jill's father, Phillip Wimple walked into the kitchen. He was talking to someone on the phone and negotiating a summer guest lecturer position at a prestigious university. He was talking about tag teaming with his wife, two for the price of one.

Her mother perked up, temporarily forgetting Jill and her problems as she heard the proposition. They were always traveling to various places to guest lecture in the summer. They had both come up with some mathematical formula that was a big deal and were basically rock stars in the academic world.

Her father especially had been super proud of that achievement. He didn't have the background like his wife, a wealthy South African family with engineers and doctors falling out of the woodwork.

Instead, he was from a different setup, his parents had been businesspeople, and Rupert and Sally Wimple had not gone to college. Instead, they started a business and had eight children together.

Sally had wanted to go to college, but she had her first child right out of high school, and that dream had been dashed. Maybe that was why she had overemphasized academia in her household.

Every one of her children had to go to college. It was non-negotiable in the family. Of her four uncles and three aunts, two were doctors, two were lawyers, two were engineers, and one was a banker.

Her father was the only one with a double doctorate and the only one in academia. Sally was fiercely proud of that.

She loved to brag about her children but would preface every conversation with—did you know that my son, Phillip, the seventh child, had a doctorate in mathematics and engineering before he was forty?

The ladies at church would nod and smile, but Jill knew they were probably tired of hearing about Sally's son Phillip with the double doctorates.

Some people lauded looks, but her family was heavy on intelligence and how smart you were. Too bad she didn't have looks nor brains.

She had said that out loud to her grandmother once, and her grandmother had looked at her and smiled.

Jill Wimple, you are a pretty girl, no doubt, but if you can't make it past a bachelor's degree, you need to marry someone with a doctorate. That way, some of the shine can rub off on you.

"What are you thinking so hard about, honey?" Her father asked. He was on hold, and he was looking over at her curiously.

"Nothing much," Jill cleared her throat.

His caller came back on the line and picked up the conversation.

Phillip Wimple was slim, tall, and fit-looking. He had a swimmer's body because that was his favorite mode of exercise. He kept his head and face cleanly shaved; his rich black skin had a natural glow to it.

He was handsome. According to her grandmother, he looked just like his father. Jill had heard numerous stories about the girls throwing themselves at him every new semester at university and how even faculty sent him naughty messages.

He only had eyes for her mother, though. The two of them were inseparable. They were high school sweethearts and shared the same nerdy obsessions.

Jill polished off the cake. Her father winked at her and gave her a thumbs up. He loved when she ate her food. For some strange reason, he thought she would be happy if she ate a lot of food. He was probably the reason she was so fat. The compulsion to please him had her eating when she wasn't even hungry.

"Can I spend the summer with Grandma Wimple in Crimson Hills?" Jill asked before her father could exit the kitchen.

"Sure," he said absently.

"No," her mother frowned. "I signed you up for the advanced summer program at our university. I signed up Ryan and Zain when they were your age."

"Mom, I suck at math and the sciences. I am not advanced in any way." Jill wailed. "I don't think I will benefit from those classes at all. I just want to spend some time with Grandma Wimple at the bakery."

"You like the bakery too much," Zara said, "it is not wise for a girl your size to be so close to pastries and sugar all summer. That is part of your problem, Jill, you are not focused on your schoolwork because you are so hyper-focused on how you look, and the more you focus on that, the more you eat and the more weight you gain.

"Academia will cure your weight issues. Look at me, thin as a rake because of it. Knowledge keeps your weight in check."

Jill didn't bother to argue with that preposterous assertation from Dr. Zara Wimple. There were plenty of fat, knowledgeable people and plenty of slim unknowledgeable ones.

She pushed away from the table and fled into her room, throwing herself on the bed. Her feet knocked the specially formulated pills off the bedside table, and she looked at them balefully. Maybe if she took the whole bottle, she would melt away into nothing because she was not academically inclined and would never get slim.

She grabbed the tablets and swallowed them one by one until the whole bottle was done.

Chapter Five

Larry jammed the headphones in his ears and continued walking briskly up the hill. He was disturbed and felt soundly rejected, if he were to be honest. Shades of summer seven years ago came back to haunt him.

All because of Jill.

Why was it that she was the one woman who affected him this way? At eighteen, he had thought it was a fluke. At twenty-five, he felt the same way. Well, not the same, maybe deeper with a hint of frustration that she wouldn't take him seriously.

He had done what she said in her little summer speech seven years ago, he had finished school, worked for a bit in the States, had several girlfriends, dated around, sowed his so-called wild oats, and now he was back.

He had gotten no real joy out of doing any of those things. Maybe if he hadn't gotten serious with Jill when he did, he would have been fine now. The trajectory of his life would have been so much different, but he had gotten serious about her and developed real feelings for her. She had changed him.

And now she was thinking of marrying another man, not just any random man, the pastor of her church. The man was opposite to him in every way. Her grandmother would be pleased. Marrying clergy had always been Sally Wimple's dream for Jill.

Sally had once called him an unprincipled philistine. All because he had told her sarcastically that some of the best Christians he knew had never stepped foot in a church. Right-doing and church-going were not necessarily compatible. He probably had been smoking at the time; marijuana had been his drug of choice. He would deliberately light up around Sally because he loved to rub her the wrong way.

He had enjoyed seeing her bristle in disdain at his very presence.

Sally had snared at him. Mark my words boy, my Jill will end up with a nice, church-going, conservative man; the higher up in the church rankings, the better. As for you, I have no clue how you will end up. Quite likely drugged up, strung out, and hopping from rehab to jail and living off your rich parents.

Larry chuckled to himself. Sally was no prophetess. He had gone to university and done well, but maybe he should have cut her a little slack. He appeared to be out of control and had unnecessarily worried his parents.

He rode his bike around the hills at breakneck speed, and he had given the middle finger to anyone in authority who had dared to question him.

He knew his mother was always requesting prayers for him at Crimson Hill Baptist Church, giving people the wrong impression of him. Additionally, when he was fourteen, the pastor at the time, Pastor Richards, befriended him. His parents had approved of the relationship and wanted it to have a calming effect on him.

Larry chuckled to himself in the half-dark. Pastor Richards hadn't befriended him out of any benevolence whatsoever. He just wanted to know who provided him with marijuana and if he could get it cheaply.

That was his first realization that pastors were not saints.

You had some who tried, but some of them were worse than criminals, and he had a pretty good handle on sussing out the bad eggs. He had a bad feeling about Rodney Charming ever since he saw him.

He wasn't one of the good ones, and Larry could feel it the moment he stepped foot in Crimson Hills.

Larry found himself heading toward the church manse, a determination to his step. He had to save Jill from herself. She couldn't marry this guy. He was not good news. And it wasn't because he was interested in Jill for himself. Tying herself to this man would be bad news. He could feel it within himself. And now he sounded like one of the church people he liked to mock. He was always highly skeptical of people who felt things within themselves, and now here he was with the same argument.

Christians called it the holy spirit. He liked to think it was just basic intuition built into our DNA to help with survival.

The churchyard was well-lit. They were having a meeting over there. He went a little further uphill to the manse; it was set back from the road quite a bit. Rows of palm trees flanked the driveway leading up to the house. The manse was in good shape. His father had voluntarily offered to fix the three-bedroom building when a freak storm had blown off the roof two years ago. The church had taken the opportunity to refurbish the whole building. Pastor Hunt, had moved elsewhere with his family. So the house had been available when Charming moved here a year ago.

There was a light in the living room.

He hoped that meant that Charming was home. Larry pressed the buzzer at the gate. When he was younger, he could walk right up to the door. Still, these were different times, probably having people walk right up to the manse had become a nuisance to whichever pastor was in residence.

"Who is it?" Charming's voice asked politely over the intercom.

"Larry Nelson," Larry said, hoping all his hostility toward this man wasn't spilling into his voice.

"Larry Nelson?" Charming sounded shocked. "Bobby and Bunny Nelson's middle son?"

"One and the same," Larry said. "I need to speak to you about Jill. I don't know what you are about Buster, but you are not…."

The side gate made a clicking sound and opened.

Larry pushed it and walked up the long driveway to the front door. Charming was standing on the veranda in jeans and a white t-shirt. It was the first time Larry saw him dressed so casually. He didn't have the usual haughty tilt to his head either. He appeared almost scared.

Larry frowned, thrown off a bit. What did he have to be scared about?

"Why did you propose to Jill?" He asked aggressively.

"Would you like to come inside?" Charming asked, looking around.

Larry shook his head. "No, this is not a social visit. I want you to be honest and tell me what you are up to, and why are you involving Jill in it?"

Charming looked at him, transfixed. "I am not up to anything. Why would you assume that?"

"Call it discernment." Larry growled, "but I have this sense that you are not to be trusted. You are hiding something, and try as I might, I can't shake the feeling."

Charming folded his arms. "That's interesting. I didn't know you understood the concept of discernment."

"That's quite the insult. You are implying that I am all brawn, no brains." Larry glared at him. "Okay, let's get something straight here, you may have the villagers fooled with your two doctorates, and you may talk a good talk, but you asked the wrong woman to marry you. I happen to care for Jill, and I am not going to just let her marry you without finding out what you are really about. Get it straight, Charming. I am not one of your church girl fans. I am about to dig up every dirt on you possible."

He spun around and headed to the gate.

"Wait!" Rodney said urgently, "I didn't know Jill was involved with someone. I wouldn't have asked her otherwise. I don't intend for this to be a real marriage."

"We are not involved." Larry turned around and said through gritted teeth. "I care about her whether she likes it or not. She thinks this will be a real marriage. All she has to do is lose one hundred pounds, and then you'll live as man and wife. I literally cannot stand the thought of it. You are giving off user vibes, taking advantage of a woman with low self-esteem."

"It's never going to happen with Jill and me." Rodney scoffed, "she'll never lose it. Jill has always been big. And even if she does lose weight by some divine miracle, I am not attracted to her. She is not my type, not even a little bit. Jill is just doing me a favor."

Larry clenched his fist. He didn't know if he should feel angry on behalf of Jill or happy about what Charming was saying.

"I thought Christians thought marriages were forever, not to be used as a gimmick or some stopgap measure. Does Jill know that this is what you are intending?"

"Not in so many words." Charming pushed his hand in his pocket and rocked back on his heels.

"So why are you leading her on?" Larry asked. "And why do you need a stop-gap? And why are you out here?"

"You ask so many questions." Charming sighed. "I never banked on having you in the background when I asked Jill to marry me."

"Too bad." Larry folded his arms. "I am very much here and am not going away."

"If I tell you this, will you please not go rummaging around in my background?"

"So there is something there?" Larry raised an eyebrow. "I knew it. What is it murder? Adultery? Stealing? Lying? Covetousness?"

Charming sighed. "So you know the last five of the ten commandments? I am going to stop underestimating you, Larry."

Larry smirked. "That would be nice, but I see you are stalling."

"I uh, it's a long story," Charming cleared his throat, "would you like a seat?"

"No, thank you," Larry shook his head, "just tell it."

"A year and a few months ago, I was the head of the university church at one of the biggest Bible Colleges in Canada. I was there for five years in that capacity, but then the president of the university announced that he was going to move on, so I and many others at the school applied for the job. It was supposed to be a shoo-in for me. I was popular with the board; I have two doctoral degrees. I just had two flaws: I was single and had developed an undeserved reputation for being a womanizer. I say undeserved because I am super picky about women and prefer to thoroughly vet each potential candidate for wife. They usually disappointed me."

Larry shook his head. "You sound like a womanizer to me."

"I can see why you would think that." Charming sighed. "I lost my heart to my brother's wife. Well, she wasn't his wife before. She just chose him over me. Ironically, because I was pursuing ministerial studies in college. No other woman has been able to take her place since, believe me, I tried to replace her. As I see it, he had the life I was supposed to be living with her."

"Family reunions must be rough for you," Larry said sarcastically.

"Well, there hasn't been much of a reunion since he married her, and there won't be any reunion now that he is dead," Charming sighed. "Anyway, back to my secret."

"My condolences. I have brothers. I can't imagine any of them not being around," Larry nodded. "Please go on."

"I was shortlisted," Charming leaned on the post and relaxed his shoulders. "I was one of three, but one of the candidates was playing dirty. He tried to jeopardize the other candidate and me by playing into our so-called weaknesses. He thought mine was girls. Probably because I dated around so much."

"Ah," Larry said. "You were a man whore. Religious man whores are the worst, pious on the outside, sexual deviants, on the inside."

Charming sighed. "Do you want to hear the rest of my story or what?"

"Go on." Larry shrugged.

"So, my competitor arranged for a particular student to

work in my office. I didn't pay her much attention until one day I went into my office after a long stressful day and found her on my desk, naked. She said she loved and wanted me and was on fire. One thing led to another.

"My defenses were down; I should have known it was a setup. I took the bait. I was saved from having outright sex with her because my secretary was working late and knocked on the door. It was the splash of cold water I needed, but it was too late. The girl recorded all of it on her phone. It looked bad; I am not gonna lie."

"Ooh," Larry whistled sarcastically, "too bad, so sad."

"Allegedly, she was also a month shy of sixteen, which is the age of consent in Canada." Charming cleared his throat. "I say allegedly because she has since disappeared. Gone from the face of the earth. I have an investigator trying to find her. I need to find her because I have criminal charges hanging over my head, and until that is clear, I can't return home. I will be arrested at the airport."

"Is that so?" Larry murmured.

"If I can prove that she is not a minor, which I suspect she was not, I will sue the university for wrongful dismissal. And if I can tie her to the now university president, I am going to sue him too for damage to my reputation. I'll leave and take up a post elsewhere when all that is sorted out. I must admit that sometimes I feel like these hills are closing in on me."

"Wow," Larry whistled. "You have a lot going on. I hope it works out for you, but you must tell Jill all this."

Charming sighed. "I know. I haven't told her, only because I didn't want her to run for the hills."

"Too bad." Larry smirked, "is there anything else you are not telling me? I believe you are hiding something."

Charming shook his head. "Maybe your sense of

discernment is sending you wrong signals."

"It never does," Larry said. "My parents always said I am a walking lie detector. It's a gift I was born with. I can sniff out a phony a mile away, and my phony radar is still active."

Charming swallowed. "Well, that is a unique gift."

"And while I don't believe you just lied," Larry said, "I think you are not telling me the whole truth."

He walked toward the gate, turned back, and gave Charming one last glare, which he doubted the man could see in the low light. Something was still not right. Maybe because he was anxious about how Jill would respond to the story. What if she wanted to marry the man anyway?

****

When Larry finally got home, Lee Wiley was waiting at the Nelson family main gate. He still was not settled in his head about Rodney Charming. There was still a disquieting feeling at the back of his mind. He could still investigate the man to find out what else he was hiding, but he wouldn't have to if Jill doesn't marry the man. He would leave him with his soap opera life to carry on and do whatever he was doing.

Lee wound down his car window.

"Where were you?" Lee asked, "I drove up and down the hills hunting for you. I eventually had to drop Dacy home. I was determined to talk to you tonight."

"I stopped to see the pastor," Larry said, "I insisted that he tell me what was going on with him, and he did tell me. I think I believe him, but something is missing."

"What's his story?" Lee asked, fascinated.

Larry told him.

Lee whistled. "So that's why he is out here. He got caught

on camera having sex with a minor."

"Alleged minor. He can't find her to confirm it," Larry said. "He lost his job and is hiding in our hills until he can resolve his situation. So why were you looking for me?"

"I wanted to discuss you helping Jill," Lee said, "whether she gets married or not, I want her to lose weight. She is motivated to do it now; I don't want to wait six months before she does something about it, so I am asking you to stand in as my proxy. I want you to be her personal trainer and cheerleader."

"I wouldn't mind." Larry shrugged. "I already told her I would help; she reacted like a scalded cat."

"Dacy said you two have history." Lee raised an eyebrow, "How deep was it?"

"First love deep," Larry said, "I don't know how she did it, but she got under my skin. I still feel vestiges of it to this day. I came back and tried to avoid her for a year, but I kept thinking that maybe what we had could be explored a bit more, but Jill had excluded me from her list of potential mates. I haven't had the time to dedicate to breaking down all of Jill's resistance, which I know how to do."

"Maybe she still feels the same way," Lee said, "but she is in denial."

"Denial, I don't think so." Larry shrugged, "I like the concept of Jill in denial over me and that one day she will realize that she loved me all the while, but that's not going to happen. Jill was indoctrinated at the feet of Sally Wimple, and Sally Wimple wanted her to be with someone conservative and pious. You can't fight that sort of socialization."

"Pastor Charming is not conservative and pious," Lee said. "He is a womanizing rat who got caught having sex with a minor."

"It doesn't matter if he is the devil himself. He has the title pastor before his name, and that gives him a wide advantage in Jill's book." Larry sighed, "I am resigned to the idea that she will go through with it regardless."

"We will do our best to talk her out of it." Lee sighed.

"You will have a better chance than I ever will. She runs when she sees me." Larry chuckled. "Apparently, I make her uncomfortable."

"Which is not necessarily a bad thing. Surely that means she still feels something." Lee murmured. "I will have to find some way for her to accept your help."

Chapter Six

"**W**ow, you look nice, Jill!" Cambria exclaimed when Jill opened the door to her living space.

"Thank you," Jill said. She had been in the process of preening in front of the full-length distorted mirror in the hallway.

Maud Beecher from Crimson Hill Great House had given her the mirror because it had made her look too slim. Jill had taken it off Maud's hands, thinking that it was just Maud being eccentric and weird as usual, but the mirror indeed had a defect.

It was warped, but in a good way, for her at least. It stretched your reflection a bit, which made it perfect. It made her appear much slimmer. She didn't mind the illusion.

Cambria walked into the apartment and chuckled. "You were looking in the magic mirror?"

"Oh yes," Jill nodded. "And I like what I see."

"You don't need it today," Cambria said cheerfully. "You

really do look fab. Larry will be impressed."

Jill grunted. "Why do you like talking about Larry so much? I am going to marry Rodney."

Cambria smirked.

Jill spun around and looked at her reflection again. She had to admit she looked good in the long v-neck white dress with the lace details she had picked up from Nessa's. Shay's mother's clothing store. It was there that she capitulated and bought the shapewear that Nessa had on sale in the plus-sized department.

At least it wasn't cutting off her circulation like the ones she had tried in the past, and it made her appear as if she had somewhat of a shape.

The dress emphasized her wide hips and gave her an hourglass profile. She had coupled that with white shoes and a gold bag. She had painted her nails gold to keep up with the white and gold theme of the party, and she had let her hair out in all its curly glory. She felt like a plus-sized young Diana Ross.

It felt good to be going to a party where she wasn't going to work. She could enjoy herself with not a care in the world.

"The caterers have already collected the cakes for Bunny's party. Mercedes came to collect the wedding cake personally for the surprise wedding between Jeremiah and Shay, and I personally saw to it that the delivery for the two kids' parties went off without a glitch," Cambria said, sitting down warily on the sofa. "The bakery is now blessedly empty and closed for the rest of the day. I am heading to Jack's for a meeting with the wedding planner my mother hired."

"I thought you were invited to Bunny's party," Jill said. "Why aren't you going?"

"Bunny plans her party a year in advance." Cambria yawned, "Jack and I were not around when she finalized her guest list. She did give me a verbal invite a few weeks ago, but I told her I had other plans. We kept putting off the wedding planner because Jack has a lot of things to deal with at the farm. Today is the day when we decide on some key things, and I didn't want to put it off again. The wedding is in sixteen weeks, and we haven't even met to discuss colors."

"I see," Jill nodded. "That's understandable."

"You'll have fun." Cambria chuckled. "Don't drink too much or dance too hard."

"I can't promise any such thing," Jill laughed, flicking her hair over her shoulders. "I don't know what the evening will bring."

****

It was a golden afternoon at the Cloud Nine Inn, Bunny's party venue. The sunlight benevolently bathed the place in golden tones, perfectly mirroring Bunny's gold and white color scheme. A mild wind blew from the sea, which was easily seen from most of the property.

Jill reached the venue just in time for the wedding segment of the party. Jeremiah had proposed, and Shay had said yes. Everybody was gathered around the white and gold decorated gazebo, and the staff was busily laying out chairs for the ceremony to begin.

"Thank you so much for making the cake." Mercedes came up to her, grinning. "I am sorry I have been of no help to you even though I offered."

Jill grinned. "I didn't expect you to do any baking, and it was no problem at all to get it done once we cleared certain things out of the way."

"I won't forget the favor," Mercedes said. "The chairs are

filling up, let's get seated, and see these two get married off before Shay changes her mind."

She hooked her hand in Jill's and led her right over to Larry.

"Uh oh," Mercedes said not quite innocently, "it's the only chair available. Can you move over, Larry, and let Jill take the aisle seat."

Larry looked up at them and smiled slowly. "Sure, anything for Jill."

"I don't want to sit beside him," Jill hissed.

Mercedes grinned. "It won't be for long. It's Larry. He doesn't bite."

She melted away into a sea of white-clothed bodies, blending in seamlessly. Jill was on her own. She sat beside Larry reluctantly.

She glanced at him; he looked good as usual. His features worked together; his level brows, short straight nose, generous pink lips, and almond-shaped eyes came together to create a compelling face that she found difficult to look away from.

But look away, she did. She was not going to get sucked into a Larry-sized obsession again. She had to have her guard up.

"You look good in white." He leaned closer to her and whispered, "I like it when you let out your hair. I remember it all over my pillow. I can't get the image out of my head."

She tried not to inhale his perfume, but she lost the battle. She shifted in her seat and glared at him. "Let's not talk to each other."

"What did you say?" He brought his lips closer to her ear, and she could feel the hot air from his breath, "I can't hear you."

Jill bit her lips. "Larry, please behave. I want to have a

relaxing time out. I can do without you whispering in my ear."

He straightened up. "Interesting. Do I still unsettle you?"

"You know you do," Jill whispered, "and I don't want that in my life right now. Can we pretend as if we don't share a past? At least for this evening."

"I can do that." Larry nodded. "Well, I guess I'll have to reluctantly introduce myself again. Hello, my name is Lawrence Robert Nelson, but everybody around here calls me Larry."

He pushed out his hand for her to shake. Jill looked at it and frowned. "My name is Jillian Wimple. Everyone around here calls me Jill."

Larry chuckled. "I have heard the surname Wimple before. Are you associated with the bakery at Crimson Hills?"

Jill sighed. "Yes, I am. You don't have to take the just meeting thing so literally."

"I am confused." Larry shrugged. "But I kind of expect it. I know of another Jill Wimple, and she confuses me too. You see, she is planning to marry a man she doesn't love and who doesn't love her, all in an effort to save him from getting fired from his job."

"Will you shut up!" Jill hissed.

"Wow, you are rude," Larry pretended to be offended. "The other Jill Wimple that I know is a really nice person. She would never growl at me and tell me to shut up."

Jill looked around to see if there were other seats available.

She spotted Dacy and Lee in the back. She waved to Dacy and was about to get up when an usher came by and handed her a program.

"Are there any empty seats back there?" Jill asked, pointing to the back.

"No," the usher smiled, "and we are about to begin."

Larry chuckled beside her, and Jill pretended as if she didn't hear him.

She swallowed a retort and opened the program. The first couple of pages had pictures of Jeremiah and Shay from their college days to now.

It was evident from their early pictures how close they were from then. And the rest of the photos were of Shay with the Nelsons and her family, the Driscolls.

Jill lingered on the pictures with the Nelson family. Bobby and Bunny Nelson had created a tight-knit family circle that was enviable.

They were so tight that Bobby was Jeremiah's best man, and Bunny was Shay's matron of honor. Granted that it was a surprise wedding, but still, Jill couldn't imagine wanting her parents to stand in that role when she got married.

Even though her family was close, they weren't as tight-knit as the Nelsons. And if the truth were to be told, Jill had always felt a little left out of her immediate family circle. Her parents and older brothers all had PhDs. When they got together, Jill always felt as if they were speaking a different language.

When they came together once or twice a year, she always felt like the odd, dumb one.

It wasn't even their fault. They tried to include her in their conversations, but all she talked about was food, and they were frankly not that interested.

All of them, including her brothers' wives, were slim and fit and mostly off sugar and had regular exercise routines. They would rather talk about cauliflower rice and the latest health fad than how to get the perfect soufflé.

She couldn't fight the underlying feeling that they pitied her for being so big or so obsessed with pastry making.

"The first step toward loving yourself is watching the

narrative in your head," Larry whispered near her ear.

Jill jumped. "How did you know what I was thinking?"

"I don't," Larry said, "I do know how much you like to get down on yourself, though, so I figured you were over there stewing about something and thinking how inadequate you were."

"I dislike you intensely," Jill muttered.

"You don't dislike me. As a matter of fact, you like me a little bit too much," Larry chuckled. "You are so hyper-aware of me; it makes you uncomfortable."

"Sexual chemistry and love or like are two different things." Jill hissed.

"At least you admit we have sexual chemistry." Larry smiled. "Which boggles the mind, the two of us are compatible in every way, and yet you've been distancing yourself from me. But, on the other hand, Charming is safe. He doesn't make your skin burn when he touches it, and he doesn't make you yearn with need when he whispers in your ear.

"And what's more, he is keeping you at arm's length. Except for the fact that he'll meet your grandmother's approval, I don't see what's the appeal. He ticks all the boxes for her, not you."

"He's also handsome and has two PhDs," Jill said. "He's a good catch. No one can deny that. And he asked me out of all the women at church."

"He is good-looking, I'll give him that. And it does take dedication to get a doctorate, and to do it twice is admirable. Still, I fail to see what value that would bring to a relationship when it comes to love, warmth, affection, and faithfulness." Larry sighed. "What did your parents say when you told them you were planning to marry him?"

"I haven't told them yet."

"Oh really, keeping secrets from your loved ones and your marriage is just two weeks away. What is it about you, people and secrets? I spoke to Charming, and he told me some whoppers the other night."

"You spoke to Rodney?" Jill widened her eyes in alarm. "Why?"

"Because I don't trust him," Larry shrugged, "your marriage plan is ridiculous. Someone has to have your best interest at heart. I went to the manse to ask him why he is really marrying you?

"He was reluctant to answer, but I threatened to go digging in his past, and it frightened him so much that he told me that he's here because he got fired from his job and was running from the law."

"That can't be true." Jill swallowed. "What utter nonsense."

"Have I ever lied to you?" Larry asked.

"Well, no. I know you prioritize honesty."

"So, what was the explanation you came up with in your head? Why would a man with two Ph.D.'s who was the head of his university church at one of the biggest Bible Colleges in Canada and who was in line to be the next president would be here in the bushes?"

"I never thought about it much," Jill said, "sometimes the Lord sends people to various places where they are needed to make a difference."

"To Christianize the heathens? Somehow, I don't think Crimson Hill has any heathens at all. Everyone is affiliated with some religion. Oh goodness," he pretended astonishment, "except me. I might be the sole heathen in Crimson Hills. I am probably the only unaffiliated person in the whole countryside. According to the modern definition of the word."

Jill frowned at him. "The modern definition?"

"Well, the word's etymology is literally dweller on the heath, one inhabiting uncultivated land, a person living out in the countryside, not the fertile type of countryside like Crimson Hills though."

"Larry." Jill said wearily, "is there a point to this?"

"Oh," Larry chuckled. "We were talking about your pastor friend and why he was fired. Let's see, he got caught on camera with a young girl. They fired him. He fled to our hills. Apparently, he chose the wrong church because Crimson Hill Baptist does not like single guys, ergo, the reason he asked you to marry him. And he asked you because Jill, let's face it, you would say yes. You have a problem with saying no to everybody else except me. You have been saying no to me since I came back, not verbally, but you have been keeping your distance."

"Stop this," Jill said weakly.

"No," Larry said. "You need to put a stop to this. I told him to tell you, but I don't know what he's waiting on."

Jill was prevented from responding. The marriage ceremony had begun. Her head was churning with the information that Larry had just landed in her lap. It was almost impossible to focus on the reverend as he spoke.

"Marriage is like a garden. It takes time to grow, but the harvest is rich unto those who patiently and tenderly care for it. If you don't cultivate it, weeds will sprout up and crush the results of your hard-earned labor…."

"Amen," Larry murmured beside her.

Jill glanced at him; he was grinning at her.

"Marriage is also like a three-legged stool. It's you, your spouse, and God. Thank God, marriage is not a hobby; it is the main job."

"Marriage should not be a rushed decision and should not

be taken lightly. It's made in heaven and consummated on Earth."

"Wow," Larry whispered. "Shouldn't you be shouting out ouch right about now?"

Jill bit her lip and closed her eyes, trying to drown out Larry.

"I admire Shay and Jeremiah," the reverend said, "I have to reluctantly say I was one of those who tried to push them into a commitment though she was not ready. Shay resisted all my attempts to push her into it, and to his credit, Jeremiah never tried to either. Shay knew the seriousness of marriage.

"When you take a vow in the presence of God, the highest spiritual being in the universe. Then you must know it is not a light commitment."

The Reverend went on and on, hitting Jill with every point he made. It was a relief when he stopped speaking, and Shay and Jeremiah could say their vows to each other.

"You may kiss the bride," the reverend said, and Jeremiah enthusiastically kissed Shay.

Larry chuckled beside her. "That's my bro."

He turned to Jill after the ceremony was over.

"Don't be foolish and marry this guy, Jill," Larry said. "You will regret it. And when you come to your senses and are ready to accept that you love me, you'll be tied up in a marriage with him. You'll be a sweet church lady on the outside but call me at night to help you relieve your sexual needs."

"You are crazy," Jill hissed. "That won't happen. We hung out for one summer."

"We did more than hang out," Larry smiled. "You were my first, and I was yours. You can't rewrite history."

"Keep your voice down," Jill said, mortified. "People make mistakes. Why can't you allow me to forget mine?"

"I don't like you thinking of us as a mistake," Larry said, "I think we should fully explore our relationship out in the open. We can go about this like mature adults. Unlike last time, your grandmother isn't here to fill your head with nonsense. We could live together for a while and see if we would like it."

"No," Jill growled. "I am a Christian woman; I have a standing in this community."

"That you wear like a talisman to ward me off." Larry sighed. "Since I've been back, Jill, you've been playing with me, and I'm getting tired of it. I was going to wait you out, but Charming is ruining my plans. He is trying to manipulate you. Ditch him. Tell him to go marry someone else for his convenience. You are just twenty-eight. What's the rush?"

"Give me strength," Jill murmured. "Marriage means a lot to me. It signals commitment. I want to be in a committed relationship. Any relationship I embark on now is with that in view."

"Okay, if that's what you want," Larry nodded, "I understand. I will marry you, then."

Jill couldn't wait to get up. "I am tired of your jokes."

"I wasn't joking." Larry said, "I would marry you just so you don't waste your time marrying that guy. Besides that, I want to make love to you again."

"Please avoid me for the rest of the evening," Jill got up, and her lips trembled. She felt like slapping him in his smug, handsome face.

"At least consider my proposal," Larry said earnestly, "I wouldn't be putting any restrictions on you for us to consummate our marriage. I am ready to go now, whatever size you are. Hell, every ten pounds you lost would be like having sex with a different woman all the time!"

Jill walked away from Larry and went smack into Dacy.

"Hold your horses," Dacy laughed, "I was coming to rescue you from Larry. For a moment there, I thought you would punch him."

"I should have," Jill growled, "but I didn't want to cause a scene."

Dacy laughed and hooked her hand into hers. "I have always said that Larry is the only human being on earth who brings out that passion in you. You turn from a fluffy kitten into a growling lioness around him. Come, let us go find drinks. You have only ten minutes to vent about Larry because I want us to have fun tonight. I haven't been to a Bunny Nelson party since forever. You know it's going to be good."

Chapter Seven

"Good, you are here!" Bunny said to Larry breezily. "I have somebody I want you to meet."

Larry looked up from a computer rendition of a layout for a house that he was trying to adjust and blinked at his mother.

"Where else would I be?"

"Knocked out from last night." Bunny chuckled. "Young people have no idea what it means to party hard from the night before and show up to work the next day as if none of it happened."

Larry chuckled. "It was a good party. I didn't enjoy myself as much as you, though. You were on the dancefloor almost all night."

"And yet here I am, ready to face the day." Bunny grinned. "Call me Energy Bunny."

"Very funny," Larry said, "I know you have at least two shots of espresso in you."

"I do," Bunny said. "By the way, thank you for the gift. I have it on right now." She waved her hand for him to see the bracelet he had given her; it had all her children and grandchild's name on it with little hearts. She had stipulated that she wanted only gold for her gifts. After all, it was her fiftieth birthday and her golden birthday milestone.

"You are most welcome," Larry said. "Where is the person you want me to meet?"

"Oh, she is in my office," Bunny said, "she is an interior designer like you. She showed up looking for a job just when I needed to give you some help with your workload. I know you have always wanted a female perspective."

"Yes, cool." Larry nodded, "we need at least two more designers if we are going to maintain our reputation of having fast turnaround on projects."

"I know." Bunny nodded. "I am working on it. We needed so many people for the Pleasant Hill project that the recruitment agency hasn't gotten around to an interior designer yet. They are not exactly a dime a dozen, you know."

"I know." Larry grinned.

"We will be short-staffed for the coming week; Jeremiah is going on honeymoon."

"Lucky guy," Larry murmured.

"He was working on Bishops Den. The new owner wanted to modernize it and turn it into apartments. The outer alterations are done. Now it's time for you to work your magic. Maybe you and Piper can work on that together."

Larry groaned. "Is this a priority?"

"Yes." Bunny nodded, "the new owner is Donovan Hendrickson. He buys properties like Bishops Den, old family monstrosities, puts a modern spin on them, and rents or resells them. We want him to have a good impression of us. He could be a repeat customer, so please, push this up in your pipeline. You can use this project to familiarize yourself with Piper's skill set. You are in charge of her."

"I am her supervisor?" Larry widened his eyes.

"Well, if we hire more people, you would head this department," Bunny said.

"I want a nameplate," Larry snickered, "and I also want a raise in pay."

"I will do the necessary updates," Bunny said without blinking an eye.

"Wow," Larry grinned, "all I had to do was ask, huh?"

"We value your work here," Bunny said. "You are creative and think of things our architects and builders haven't considered. You are solely responsible for the compliments we've been getting lately. It has not gone unnoticed by me or Bobby. And surely you must realize that more people are coming to you to ask for your opinion."

"I noticed," Larry said, "it is quite the vindication for me. You and Dad used to think I wouldn't be a contributing member of society."

"I never once thought that," Bunny protested, "I have always held out hope that you would grow out of your middle child syndrome."

"You sound like Mercedes," Larry frowned, "I never had middle-child syndrome."

"You were a textbook middle child. You thought we didn't love you, you acted out to get attention if we said left, you went right. We had to be so careful with you, we may have been a little bit too lenient, and I did question my parenting skills with you more than I did the other children, but it had never entered my mind that you wouldn't find your way in the end."

Bunny smiled. "I think I have Jill to thank for turning you

around at eighteen."

"Jill?" Larry raised his brow. "Why her?"

"When you 'secretly' started seeing her, you changed," Bunny chuckled. "She turned my rebel into a man who became serious about his future and reputation. You stopped smoking and cursing. You became more respectful and reachable. And you didn't tattoo your face as you were threatening. I will always be grateful to Jill for that."

Larry snorted. "I guess she did have some influence on me."

"Oh, she did. No guessing about it." Bunny nodded. "And she still is. Aren't you doing a doctorate in civil engineering just because of her?"

"Mom, I told you and Dad that I was doing my Ph.D. in confidence. Why are you bringing it up casually in conversation?" Larry hissed. "Have you told anyone?"

"No," Bunny shrugged, "but aren't you finishing up in six months? And won't people know when I throw a party for you then?"

"No parties. I don't want anyone to know about it." Larry growled. "And I don't want a party for my birthday either. I don't like parties."

"That's odd, you have half of my genetic material, and you hate parties," Bunny mused. "I will respect you wanting to keep your doctorate a secret but not your birthday. I am throwing one for you this year, you only turn twenty-six once, and you haven't been around for most of the last seven years. I am going to go ham with this one.

"Anyway, back to business," Bunny said before Larry could protest. "Let me go get Piper and the Bishop's Den file. You two need to get acquainted. Oh, and when you are headed up to the Bishops Den, please drop off this envelope by Jill for me." Bunny handed him an envelope.

"She deserves a tip for those cakes she did. They tasted good and were decorated so beautifully, I was reluctant to cut them."

****

Larry didn't know what to make of Piper Miller. She was younger than he thought she would be and quite pretty. She had her hair slicked back in what should be a severe hairstyle, but it only emphasized her high cheekbones and the delicate arch of her eyebrows.

She was tall and modelesque and was dressed in a tailored pants suit that looked both sophisticated and businesslike at the same time.

She was subdued at first, but after the first couple of minutes, where both of them sized each other up and she showed him her skills with the design software, he realized she was not reserved at all.

She was gregarious and outgoing, and flirty. He didn't like the flirty part. After the umpteenth time of her reaching across to touch him or bat her eyelashes at him. He had to put a stop to it.

"Listen, Piper, I am not interested in anything but a strictly business relationship. If you don't stop touching me, I will report you to HR for sexual harassment."

Piper laughed uncomfortably, "are you serious?"

"Yes, keep it professional with me," Larry said. "You and I will get along just fine if we respect each other's boundaries."

"I am so sorry," Piper said, chastened. "I am the one always making that speech. I am mortified."

"Forget about it," Larry said. "We now have an understanding. Let's just get on with it."

He made an appointment with Donovan Hendrickson to meet him at the previously named Bishops Den at eleven, and he and Piper set off on their first assignment together.

"I have never been to Crimson Hills," Piper said excitedly when she sat in his car. "I only heard about it recently because Dacy Bishop was falsely incarcerated for killing her brother, and she was released from prison. I was so happy for her. I cried because of the injustice of it all. Do you know her?"

"Oh yes, her name is Dacy Granston though, she wasn't an acknowledged Bishop while growing up." Larry nodded. "The house where we are going now is where the murder supposedly took place."

"I still can't believe that sort of thing happened in real life." Piper sighed. "Do you know if Olivia Bishop was charged for anything?"

"Yes, she was," Larry nodded, "accessory to insurance fraud, I think. She and her son, Peyton, are currently in court."

"And nothing may come of it," Piper shook her head. "The hands of justice in this country moves a little bit too slowly for me. My cousin's husband's company was involved in some fraudulent dealings in the US. He wasn't even one of the key players. He was just an accountant doing his job. Next thing you know, they froze his assets and practically declared everything my cousin jointly owned with him as proceeds of a crime. They hit them hard and hit them quickly. And right when she had quit her job too because she had just had a miscarriage. The frozen assets hit her hard. And hit them where it mattered."

"But freezing of assets is not permanent," Larry said.

"I know," Piper widened her eyes dramatically, "the government froze the assets until the trial was over."

"So, was he prosecuted?" Larry asked.

"No," Piper sighed, "he never had a chance to answer the charges. He went to Canada to meet up with his brother and died in a car accident."

"That's sad." Larry said, "he should have gotten the chance to defend himself in court."

"Maybe or maybe not," Piper murmured, "all the accountants, in that case, got convicted on several counts of fraud. The longest jail time was fifteen years. I tell you, my cousin Lailah was so devastated when he died, but she would have lost him to ten to fifteen years in jail if he had survived the accident, no doubt about it. He was the main accountant at that firm, and the higher-ups were setting him up to be the fall guy."

"Lailah," Larry whispered, "where have I heard that name before?"

"It rhymes with Lilac," Piper grinned, "which is almost the name that my aunt and uncle called her."

"No, that's not it," Larry drummed his fingers on the steering wheel, "I was talking to Charming the other night, and he mentioned that he was in love with a woman named Lailah. That's where I heard it from."

"Charming?" Piper gasped.

"Yeah," Larry nodded. "It is actually a surname. I thought I had heard it all, and then Charming came on the scene. It's quite a name, isn't it? Right out of fairytale land. Maybe that is one reason why I don't like the man. His surname is literally Charming."

"I know it's a surname. That's my cousin, Lailah's, surname. She married Roderick Charming."

"Did he have a brother named Rodney Charming?" Larry asked.

"He did!" Piper nodded, "I think that's his name. They

were identical twins too. Lailah always said they so closely resembled that she couldn't tell them apart back in college. When she went back for her masters, she met the Charming brothers, and she was dating both of them and didn't know it at first."

Larry laughed. "I could see myself doing that with a twin brother. When did she find out?"

"When things started to get serious, and she arranged to meet one of them at their shared apartment off campus. She wanted to clear up some of the confusing things she thought he was telling her and how rapidly his personality had changed. Apparently, Rodney was serious and thoughtful, and Roderick was more outgoing and jovial."

"Ah," Larry nodded. "Same face, different personalities."

"They added to the confusion by using the name, Rod. Both of them told her to call them Rod." Piper chuckled. "When she showed up at the door, Rodney was on his way out, and she was confused. Didn't he know she was coming by?"

"He paused to ask her though what she was doing there? And after insisting that they made a date. He figured out what happened, and that Lailah was in the dark about his twin's identity. Rodney started to marshal her away from the house. Roderick looked outside when it was happening and opened the door and stopped them."

"Lailah was understandably shocked and confused. When it was all cleared up, they both offered to date her and waited for her to make a choice. She did that for a while, but she said she chose Roderick purely because Rodney was building his career in religion, and Roderick was transitioning out of it. He went into accounting. That was more her speed. She was doing her master's in economics."

"It's a small world because Rodney Charming is a pastor

at our local Baptist church." Larry stopped in front of Wimples Bakery. "I am going to drop this off to Jill per my mother's request."

"I am coming with you," Piper exited the car. "This spot smells so good. I didn't have breakfast this morning. I might have to get a coffee and something to eat."

"Okay." Larry looked at his watch. "We have twenty minutes. You may have to eat in the car."

Jill was at the cash register when he entered the store. He didn't expect her to be there.

"I like it in here!" Piper was exclaiming. "It's perfect and quaint, I could see myself spending time here just sitting in one of those nooks, having a coffee and looking out at the scenery. I wonder who did the design."

Jill glared at him. He expected that she that she would put up barriers between them because of their shared past, and maybe he had spooked her at the party the night before. He didn't want to ask her to marry him the way he did, and he understood why she would take it as an insult. However, after his flippant marriage offer had left his mouth, he realized that he had meant it.

He would happily marry Jill, and it wasn't to save her from marrying Rodney Charming. He would marry her for himself because as much as his pride smarted from her obvious rejection of him, his heart was still into Jill.

While he was ruminating about his unusual admission to himself, Jill was smiling at Piper. "My grandmother Sally Wimple designed the bakery. She wanted it to feel like a homely place, where you can rest for a while."

"I see," Piper contemplated the menu. "She had design skills. This place does feel homely and welcoming."

Larry looked at Jill, who was looking between him and Piper, a confused look on her face. "Hello Jill, this is Piper, our newest staff member at Nelson Construction."

Jill widened her eyes. "Oh."

Larry smiled. He could see jealousy in their beautiful brown depths. Usually, he would fan the flames, but he didn't want to play games with Jill anymore. Anything he did now could make her go careening into the arrangement with Charming. He was hoping that she wouldn't do that.

He decided to be casual and not overly friendly. "My mom sent this for you." He handed her the envelope.

"She already paid me," Jill looked up at him.

"You know, Bunny. She appreciated your hard work." Larry shrugged. "I am just the messenger."

Jill took the envelope from him and smiled. "I do know, Bunny. Are there any cakes left?"

"Not even a smidge of a slice. She gave them away as gifts." Larry shrugged. "You enjoyed yourself last night? I saw you dancing up a storm with Dacy and talking and giggling. You separated the woman from her husband and unleashed him on us."

Jill smiled. "I didn't feel bad about it. Lee was having fun his way, and so were we. I think you are bitter about it because he kept beating you guys at the domino tables."

"He was on a roll. There was no one who could beat him last night. At one point, Derrick went home for his own personal dominoes to see if he could get a game in."

Jill laughed. "I didn't even see that."

"I know," Larry said, "you were surrounded by your girl group and laughing up a storm."

Piper snapped her finger. "Wimple! Oh my God, I know why the name seems so familiar."

Jill looked across at her. "Where?"

"We went to the same prep school," Piper said. "You left after that stunt that Edgar pulled at the club meeting. He used you as the before and me as the after!"

Jill gasped.

"You are Piper Miller?"

"In the flesh," Piper said, "I have always wanted to tell you how sorry I was for being a part of that charade. I genuinely didn't know how much that little stunt would have hurt you. We heard that you wouldn't come back to the school because of how cruel we were."

Jill swallowed. "I didn't like myself much then."

"Nevertheless," Piper said, moving closer to Jill. "I am sorry about all that happened from the bottom of my heart. You were always such a pleasant person. And I think you were unfairly targeted at school."

"It was so many years ago. I barely remember that" Jill's voice cracked, "I moved here to live with my grandmother, and I love Crimson Hills so much. It's a lovely neighborhood, wonderful people."

She glanced at him and then away.

She was lying about not remembering. Larry thought sympathetically. He remembered her telling him that she had considered suicide after that and had taken a bunch of pills.

And she was feeling uncomfortable talking about that time in her life.

He decided to help her out. "Come on, Piper, we are running out of time for our appointment. You'll have to eat in the car."

Piper quickly ordered, and they hastened out of the store. But not before Larry looked back at Jill. Tears were in her eyes, and she tried to resist looking at him fully before he noticed them.

It tugged at his heart. He would have to come back later and make sure she was okay. But knowing Jill, she would probably put on the mantle of niceness and pretend as if everything was just fine.

But he would power through. He needed to tell her about Lailah. Charming's so-called one true love, and he needed to tell her about Charming's twin brother and how criminality ran through the Charming brother's veins. At least that should make her reconsider marrying the pastor.

Chapter Eight

It was raining by the time Jill closed the store. She was doing so later than usual. She had to walk to the side entrance, though, to feed her twelve outdoor cats. They lived in her two hundred square feet gardening space. There was a Julie mango tree in the middle, with a bench underneath. It had a tiny lawn, and her grandmother's hibiscus collection. There were so many different eye-popping colors and sized hibiscus.

At one time, Sally used to pot and sell them as a side business because people often asked about them. But Jill had zero time in that. The cute little potting shed, in which Sally used to spend her days off, was now a full-time cat residence. Jill had retrofitted it so that each cat had their own bowl and sleeping nook.

They could come and go as they pleased from the shed into the garden, but they couldn't go out onto the road anymore. She had meshed them in.

Now and again, her gardener, Sterling Silver, would leave the side gate open because he was forgetful, especially when he had a hangover, but they didn't go far. Her once stray cats were pampered members of her family.

Sally had started naming them after food and drinks, and Jill had continued the tradition. She knew all of them by name and personality. The oldest was Marmalade, her orange tabby. Then there was Mocha, Cookie, Pudding, Taffy, Brownie, Muffin, Cocoa, Honey, Donut, Sprinkles, Oreo, and Hershey.

Muffin greeted her at the door when she opened it. She had expected him or Cocoa to be vocal because she was late, and they were cooped up together because of the rain.

"Sorry I am late," she announced to her gang of feline friends. "I had the worst day."

Several cats came and pressed up on her legs. "You would never believe it." She headed for the cupboard where the tin food was stored.

"First off, I tried calling Pastor Charming, you know, the man I am supposed to marry as a favor so that the church doesn't kick him out?"

Her cats started meowing in earnest. Jill pretended that they were responding to her marriage news. "And I couldn't get him. I thought he would have been at Bunny's birthday bash last night, but he wasn't there, and I didn't want to ask Bunny if he was invited. That wouldn't be de rigueur, would it?"

Pudding stretched on her legs and meowed loudly.

"You don't know what de rigueur is?" Jill widened her eyes dramatically, "I thought you did, Miss Pudds."

Pudding clawed her leg, and Jill was thankful that she wore jeans.

"All right already, the word is French for etiquette, custom, the proper thing to do."

Pudding yawned.

Jill chuckled. "So where was I? Oh, the party. Then when I got there," Jill said, counting out the tins, half a tin for each cat. "I sat beside Larry, who, by the way, offered to marry me. That's after he said we could live together. Why would he even suggest something like that to me? I don't have the personality to turn up my nose at people like he does and say to hell with the rules.

"A little part of me wishes though that I was like that, maybe for a day. A Jill without rules or limitations. What would I do?"

One of her cats, Oreo, wound himself around her leg. He had patches of black and white on him, just like the cookie.

Jill sighed and looked at him. "Your mother was a friend of Larry's, you know. The only human she would go to. She was such a beautiful feline, jet black with eyes like jade. She was a rebel cat. She always had an underlying wildness. She was adventurous, and sure of herself. I guess she sensed the same in Larry."

Oreo looked at her and slightly nodded like he understood.

"I will always be attracted to Larry," Jill said morosely. "For a minute, when he had so casually proposed, I felt like saying yes and calling his bluff. But it wouldn't have come to anything, would it? He only offered to marry me so that I wouldn't marry Pastor Charming."

She took down the twelve cat plates, and her cats went to their places. It was a ritual they were used to.

She started with Marmalade, aka Marms, who was the elder in the tribe. Sprinkles and Honey, her Siamese cats, could be depended on to get impatient, but otherwise, from that, they were fairly obedient and waited their turn.

She had to work quickly, though.

"So where was I?" She shared the cat food and sat on one of the rocking chairs, watching them as they ate.

Her grandmother had decorated one half of the shed to look like a living room, with two armchairs and a sofa.

"Oh, we were talking about Larry." Jill mused. "I do talk about him a lot, don't I?

"Especially since he came back, all handsome and hunky and even more desirable. That sounds shallow, I know; I judge people based on size just like everybody else. What if Larry had come back fat and sloppy? Would I still like him?"

Marms looked up at her knowingly. She was a female ginger, which was quite rare, and maybe because of the rareness, Jill felt as if she was a notch more intelligent than the rest.

She didn't know if that was true or if she should be ascribing human personalities to her felines, but she did it all the time.

"I am torn about Larry. I know we could have something going but would it last? I could throw caution to the wind and go on a wild ride with him. And we all know it would be wild. The summer we spent together was the best summer of my life. But at the end of the day, what then?

"I could do this the respectable way, get married to a pastor, lose the weight, and then have a normal sedate relationship with him. It would be stable and predictable and lacking in excitement, but you remember what Grandma always said, the slower the fire builds, the longer it lasts. And who knows, I could develop a yearning for Rodney later on. It's not impossible."

Brownie came and sat on her lip and proceeded to lick himself. Brownie was the ultimate lap cat. He would even sleep on your head if you let him.

Brownie looked up at her mid-lick and meowed.

"It is possible," Jill caressed the top of his silky head. Brownie was a wonderful combination of dark brown fur with green eyes. He butted her hand for even more caresses and started purring.

"However, I will have to get an explanation for what Larry said to me the other night. I cannot fathom that what he said could be right. And I am not going to, under any circumstances, take the traditional wedding vows after that talk that the reverend gave at Shay and Jeremiah's wedding about marriage. I am not repeating those vows to a man I don't know yet.

"Do you think that is a good idea?"

She asked Marms, who came to sit on one handle of the rocking chair.

"Meow," Marms said.

Jill nodded. "So I shouldn't do it?"

Marms got up and stretched and then shook her head.

"Ah, so you are saying I would be making a mistake like Larry said?"

Marms looked at her and then yawned. You are boring me with your questions, was the attitude from Marms.

Jill chuckled, and Marms jumped off the armchair and headed back to her plate.

Her other cats finished eating and, one by one, came to sit around her. Oreo became fascinated with the scent of her hair and kept rubbing himself on it. She let out her hair so he could have better access, only because she intended to wash it later. She didn't have time to be picking cat hair from her curls.

He had a purr-fest around her head.

Jill sighed. Surely, she couldn't marry a man who was wanted for statutory rape. She shouldn't be thinking of marrying someone who only wanted them to have a real marriage after she lost a hundred pounds. Her dreams of proving to her parents and grandparents that she had a come-up and could pull a man with two doctoral degrees was quickly fading.

And what about Larry? And his new coworker, Piper? A shaft of jealousy hit her like it did today when she had suddenly seen Piper Miller in the flesh.

The Piper Miller, the 'it' girl, the girl she had so desired to be when she was younger, walking in with Larry into her bakery looking like she had only grown prettier.

She reminded herself, just like she had before, that she had no reason to be jealous of Piper Miller or Larry Nelson or Piper with Larry.

Larry could see who he wanted and work with whomever. It was just ironic that the girl who had been held up as the after to her before was around now at this stage of her life and working with the one man that made Jill's heart race. The one man that she secretly still had feelings for. Maybe she shouldn't have pushed Larry away this past year.

She remembered the first time she had seen him after seven whole years…

****

A year ago…

"I heard that the demon spawn of Bobby and Bunny Nelson is back." Sally Wimple said.

They were clearing out the display cases for the night. "It has been seven years; I wonder how many times he has been in rehab and how many sexually transmitted diseases he has."

"Grandma!" Jill gasped in horror. Her grandmother only degenerated into a judgmental, mean-spirited critic when it came to Larry.

It was a strange sight to see, Sally was back in Jamaica for her annual trek from visiting all her family over the world.

Somehow, Jill had hoped that in her travels that she had loosened up a bit, especially when it came to Larry. Jill was the only one of her twenty-two grandchildren that was still toeing the line, going to church, and taking it seriously.

"You have eight children and twenty-two grandchildren," Jill said patiently, "one of them is in rehab, and who knows who has STDs. Are they the devil's spawn?"

"Still defending him, huh?" Sally frowned. "I just said that to see where your head space is at where it concerns him."

"I doubt that," Jill snorted. "You are still as judgmental as ever when it comes to Larry. I have no idea why. Everybody else in this neighborhood can get a pass, but not Larry."

"He took your innocence," Sally said, "it should have been reserved for a nice Christian man in the confines of holy matrimony."

"And that will guarantee that I would live happily ever after with not a care in the world," Jill said snarkily. "Grandma, you hated Larry before that. And he didn't take anything. We had sex. It happens. Half of your grandchildren were not born in the confines of wedlock, and half of the twenty-two is from one of your sons. Uncle Oliver chases anything in a skirt. It is so bad, my dad says he doesn't want me in the same room with him. How is that for a fantasy?"

Sally sighed. She preferred to ignore the sore points in her own family. "All I am saying, Jill, is that you are special. Your destiny isn't to be with a man like Larry. You should aim high. Strive for a man with a high set of morals, a righteous man, a man who is beyond reproach, a man of high degree."

"What's wrong with Larry's morals?" Jill asked, confused. "When he comes back every year, he spends his vacation building houses in that charity with Jeremiah. They give people actual houses to live in for free. They help the homeless, and when those people are housed, they donate toward their children's education and medical fees. They do not announce what they do, Grandma. It's the people who they help that talk."

"How do you think that the Silver family in our own neighborhood could even stand a chance with drunken Sterling Silver always spending whatever money they have on booze. Garwin Silver told me that one day his father was about to kill him in a drunken rage, and Larry was the one who saved him.

"Why do you think about that when you go off on Larry. Your friend, Betty Moses, from church disagrees with you. She told me when I visited her that Larry and I were the only ones to visit her. At the time, he was sixteen. Larry was being more Christian than all of Crimson Hill Baptist church put together. You judge Larry wrongly!"

Jill didn't even realize she was shouting; Sally looked at her in stunned astonishment. Jill had never raised her voice at her before.

"What's gotten into you?" Sally asked, genuinely puzzled.

"I am single, fat, and heading towards thirty with not even one man on the horizon." Jill said, "I get passionate about you saying stuff about the one man who actually found me attractive and loved me. There is nothing wrong with Larry."

Sally sighed. "Oh Jill, I am sorry. And maybe I do go too far in trying to ward you off, Larry. I don't say the best things about him. I don't really think he is the devil's spawn."

"You don't?" Jill raised an eyebrow.

"Of course not." Sally sighed. "I have been bad-mouthing him for years in hopes that you will stay away from him because I want you to marry a pastor. You are such a good, smart girl. You would make the perfect first lady for some church, and you do look good in a hat, slanted just right. You would sit at the front as he preaches, and you would have two perfect children, and you will be happy."

Jill giggled. She didn't mind the imagery. She had that fantasy over the years, especially after she imagined what Larry was up to in college and how he was living his life.

She knew Larry's lifestyle would have nothing to do with church because Larry would never be religious. She had convinced herself to move on from him mainly for that reason.

"I think that Pastor Charming would be just right for you," Sally said. "He has the right amount of handsome, he is personable and sweet, and he preaches the best sermons, and most of all, he has two PhDs. Two PhDs like my Phillip. I didn't know there was a man who could rival your dad's two doctorates."

Jill leaned on the stone accent wall that led toward the kitchen and smiled. "He is perfect."

"If you married him," Sally said, salivating, "I would be over the moon happy. I would sign over the bakery to you as a wedding gift."

"Grandma," Jill gasped, "that's serious."

"I willed it to you anyway," Sally said, "it's technically yours. You have expanded the operation significantly. No one can argue with me about that."

"I know." Jill nodded. "But that's a serious gesture to pin to me marrying Pastor Charming. It won't happen anyway. Men like Pastor Charming don't marry women like me."

"He doesn't know what he is missing." Sally chuckled,

"you are an awesome person. I am going upstairs, I am going to pack, and off to Canada I will be going for six months. Your aunt Alice is too career-focused to spend much time with those children of hers, I am going to have to lend a hand."

"I'll follow. I am going by the shed," Jill said, "I have to feed the cats."

Sally nodded. "You are overfeeding them, Jill. Marms looks like a small lion. Maybe you should put them on a diet and then join them. It can't hurt."

"I am tired of diets," Jill rolled her eyes. "Besides, the vet visited the other day and said they are just fine and healthy."

She closed up the store and was heading for the side gate when Larry had just casually walked by.

She was the one who had stopped and done the dramatic gasp.

Larry had looked unruffled and inexplicably gorgeous. He was taller, broader, and looked like a manlier, more handsome version of the boy she had last seen.

She had stubbornly refused to see him when he came back on his vacations over the years, and he had kept a low profile. He hadn't stopped by the bakery even once, so seeing him now was something of a shocker.

"Jill," he stopped walking. He didn't crack a smile; he didn't say anything else.

"Lar…Larry," Jill stuttered. "You are back."

"For good," Larry said. "How are you?"

"I am good," Jill whispered. "How are you?"

After an awkwardly long pause, when she thought he wasn't going to answer, Larry answered. "I've been better. I came back with a cold and just trying to clear my head. I'll see you around."

He continued walking.

"Okay," Jill's heart, which had started to race, refused to settle down long after she could no longer see him going up the hill.

A part of her slumped inside. He didn't like her anymore. So this is what it felt like to face an ex. A person you still had feelings for though trying hard to forget. She felt deflated and crushed. She had stayed in the potting shed for hours and howled out her misery to her cats.

****

She was doing the same now. Except now, things were vastly different. Larry was working with Piper.

Piper had been gorgeous as ever and still slim and sleek. Larry would prefer her to Jill, of course. Even today, he had been distant when he entered the store. He had stopped flirting with her to get her attention or a reaction from her. It was well and truly over.

She felt a sharp pang of aloneness. Over the past year, she had liked the attention from Larry, their sparring back and forth, and his reminders about their past. Though she didn't think he was serious, at least he had made her feel desirable. If he had been serious, he would have made a move, but he never did.

But now, with Piper around, she would be placed on the back burner of his life, where she had always thought that she belonged anyway.

Jill sighed. She had six chocolate-covered donuts today after they left the bakery. This did not bode well for her future weight loss efforts.

Even more of a reason to tell Rodney that she couldn't do it. But something gave her pause. What if this was her only chance to claim that she was a wife, even without the regular activities that went with being married?

She didn't want to be a spinster at fifty. She didn't want to be everybody's aunty Jill, who was never married and perennially single, with only her cats for company. They already had one lady like that at church; Crimson Hill Baptist did not have space for two.

Chapter Nine

At Willie's request, Rodney visited Maud Beecher at Crimson Hill Great House. According to Willie, Maud asked for him and said it was urgent. What Maud needed was a good psychologist, Rodney thought, not a pastor. The stories she told, and her so-called time traveling was too fantasy-like for him.

He would have told that to Willie, when he came to his door, hat in hand, and declaring that Maud needed him right now before he made another move. But Rodney had been in the process of finding a minister who would wed him and Jill without asking too many questions.

He was resentful that Maud Beecher was asking him to drop everything he was doing and follow her bidding.

He was about to tell Willie that, but Willie said he wasn't budging until he came along at Maud's request.

Maud was sitting on the front steps of the great house, staring somberly in the distance when he drove up. She looked as if she was talking to herself.

"What is she saying, Willie?" He asked softly.

Willie inclined his head. "Something to do with Gemini and you."

"Gemini?" He raised his brow. "As in the star sign?"

"Yes, pastor," Willie nodded. "Maud said you were one part of a Gemini and that you are a deceiver like the devil."

Rodney recoiled physically.

Taking a step back from the woman on the steps. He had heard the stories about her, how she claimed to time travel, and how she predicted a lot of things for the future. He hadn't really had a talk with her before this.

Willie was a faithful churchgoer, but Maud avoided church like the plague. Well, she avoided it since he arrived in Crimson Hills. She had been a regular attendee before then.

Maud turned and looked straight at him then. "Hello, Pastor Charming."

She spoke, and her voice was conversational and calm. There was nothing eery about it.

"Hello, Maud," he said cautiously. "Willie said you needed me, and that it was urgent."

"Yes," Maud got up, brushed herself off, and came toward them. "I was wondering if I should intervene. I rarely do. I usually watch things play out."

Rodney was confused. He didn't know what the woman was blathering about.

She looked at him and sighed. "Your lawyer is looking in the wrong direction. I will give you a clue to save time. Tell the lawyer on your case that the girl who accused you of wrongdoing is in the province of Manitoba. Her name is Rose."

Rodney frowned. "How do you know I have a lawyer and

a case?"

"Do you really want me to spell out everything I know?" Maud asked him aggressively.

Rodney took a step back. "No."

"I also called you here to warn you. You had better not try to marry Jill Wimple for real." Maud pointed at him. "She is not for you. I do not see you here in the future with her."

Rodney swallowed. "You know about that?" He looked across at Willie, who shrugged as if to say, she knows everything.

"There is a man, Louis Green, who lives over in Cascade Hill. He is a con man; he can do your mock wedding. He doesn't have the credentials. Anything you sign will not be legal."

"Excuse me," Rodney sputtered.

Maud looked at him hard.

Fear, pure and simple, gripped him. He felt like a little boy at the principal's office. In that long hard glare, he felt somehow that she knew all his secrets. He didn't know how she knew, but she did.

He lowered his gaze from her piercing stare. "Okay."

Maud smiled at him coldly. It didn't reach her eyes. "Our time of reckoning will come. We all have our time of reckoning. You will get away with your deeds. Unfortunately, I can't get away from mine."

With that cryptic statement, she left him and went up the Great House steps.

Willie looked at him with confusion in his eyes.

Join the club, buddy, Rodney wanted to say. He cleared his throat. "Do you know who Louis Green is?"

"Yes," Willie said, "I did some work for his grand-uncle just the other day. Wait here. I have his number."

Willie went all the way to the cottage at the back and then

returned with a piece of paper bag, something was scribbled on it.

"We like Miss Jill around these parts," Willie said gruffly. "Don't even think of breaking her heart."

Rodney nodded. "I won't."

And he meant it. He would not give Jill a sliver of a chance to fall in love with him. He desperately needed her help, and she obviously needed his.

On his way to Jill's house, he called his lawyer, Michael Evans.

"You won't believe this, man," he said when the lawyer answered, "but I just spoke to a woman. Don't ask me how she knows this, but she says that you should look in Manitoba, and the girl's real name is Rose. She didn't give a surname."

Michael didn't laugh as he thought he would. "My investigator suggested Manitoba some time ago. Rose, you said?"

"Yes," Rodney said, feeling breathless.

"Who is this woman that gave you the lead?" Michael asked.

"A woman who knows my secrets without me telling her anything," Rodney murmured.

"An obeah woman?" Michael laughed, "don't you preach against those people in the pulpit?"

"She's not an obeah woman," Rodney said. "She claims that she time travels. One story I heard was that she meets up herself in various rooms in the Great House and tells herself secrets. I don't know; I can't keep track of the stories. All you need to do is check for Rose in Manitoba."

"That's a weird place you are staying at, but I will do it," Michael said. "How is everything going?"

"I have to get married to keep my position here." Rodney

sighed. "It is degrading how these country bumpkins are dictating my life."

"Who are you going to marry?" Michael asked. "And what about Lailah?"

"I found a girl," Rodney said. "I thought she was perfect for it. She is fat, kind of desperate for male attention, or so I thought. Since I proposed, and she said yes. Everybody is coming out of the woodwork, threatening me. I had no idea she had so much support."

"She has a young suitor named Larry and a couple of friends who can make my life difficult. I regret choosing her, but there is nobody else in these hills suitable for a fake marriage, in my opinion. I can easily resist Jill, and she is discrete."

"It isn't going to be a real marriage, is it?" Michael asked, "I mean, under the circumstances, you don't want to get tied up with someone else when your plans are to clear your name, propose to Lailah, sue the school and take back your rightful place."

"I was actually thinking of doing something real and then springing for a quickie annulment," Rodney said, "but the same woman I was telling you about, Maud Beecher, told me that Jill was not for me. And that I should use a con man, someone who did not have a license to perform the ceremony. She even gave me a name."

"Good," Michael said. "We don't want your life to get too complicated."

"As if it could," Rodney said. "Call me when you have anything promising. I am dying to leave this place. I want to go somewhere else and do something else. I am tired of being Pastor Rodney Charming with the two PhDs."

He stopped at the bakery and got out. Obviously, it was closed for the day. Jill was upstairs. He could see a light on up there. He would have to come clean with her and tell her the same story he told Larry and beg and plead with her to marry him. Maybe he would have to sell it as a pre-wedding wedding. He already used that line of argument.

But what was he doing out here dithering about approaching Jill?

It was Jill.

Jill was, at heart, an insecure softie who couldn't say no to save her life. Maybe he should call the Louis Green guy and move it up to tomorrow. It would give her less time to change her mind and for her various friends to meddle, and it would buy him some time.

Chapter Ten

This is a huge mistake, Jill thought throughout the five-minute ceremony. She was groggy from last night when Rodney had come to her apartment, laid out his story, and begged for her help.

She had said yes. Of course, she had. He had tears in his eyes when he told her about the injustice of losing his place at the university where he had worked for most of his adult life, all because of one female's devious actions. Jill had imagined what if it were her father who had almost succumbed to a honey trap.

By the time Rodney had laid it all out on the line, she had readily said she would help. He didn't have to assure her that he would take things slow and that they could get to know each other at their own pace.

She hadn't anticipated that he would call her the morning after. She hadn't even had her first cup of coffee yet. The officiant was in Rodney's office. His uncle, Noel, and his wife, Jane, were also on the premises. They could sign the documents as witnesses, their vows would be as generic as ever, and they would not mention God.

Jill had been adamant about that. She was not promising anything before God until she was ready. As far as she was concerned, this was purely to help out Rodney. When she said her proper vows, she would mean them.

She would say the traditional wedding vows when it was time, brightly and boldly, in front of a bunch of family and friends. By that time, she would be one hundred pounds lighter, and she would know Rodney Charming, better than she did now.

She couldn't pledge to be his wife before God and man in all good conscience. Besides, the vows and the ceremony were not what made you legally a husband or wife. The signed documents were.

The officiant was a man named Louis Green, who coughed through the duration of the ceremony. Why he spluttered and hemmed and hawed over the simple vows was a mystery to Jill.

"Say after me," he turned to Jill: "I vow to honor and respect you for all you are and will become, taking pride in who we are, separately and together. And I promise to challenge you and to accept challenges from you. I will join with you and our community in an ongoing struggle to create a world we all want to live in, where love and friendship will be recognized and celebrated in all their many forms."

Jill repeated after him because it sounded doable and realistic, not phony, and was as generic as possible.

Rodney repeated the same thing in not so many words. Louis Green probably had full-blown flu. Not one sentence of his was coherent as he mumbled through the proceedings. It was a relief when he pointed on the dotted line for Jill to sign, and then it was blessedly over.

Jill didn't feel married or particularly changed. What she felt was a niggling stomach burn from the six donuts and leftover spicy jambalaya that she had eaten the night before. They were not jiving well in her stomach.

If someone had told her that she would get married in a stuffy church hall, on a Wednesday morning, with no friends or family around, and that she would be wearing her most flattering black skirt and a white top which made her look mumsy, she would laugh them to scorn.

Her vision had always been to get married in church. She would be dressed in white, in a princess-style gown. Her hair would be in a curly chignon with bridal flowers in her hair. She would adhere to all the little traditions, and all her family and friends would be around. Her parents would be pleased with her groom. They would admit that she had done them proud. Her handsome groom would have love shining in his eyes as he looked at her. And she couldn't look away from him.

In her fantasies, the groom had always been Larry.

She had to change that. In a couple of months, she would be marrying Rodney again. And in that time, she would lose a hundred pounds, and she would get to know him better and fall knee-deep in love with him. She had to; he was now her husband.

She looked at him. He smiled widely at her. Mission accomplished for him.

"I guess we need to have a semblance of living together, or people will talk," Rodney said after the officiant had left the office.

Jill shook her head. "I am not moving."

"At least spend Sundays with me at the manse." Rodney urged. "After church, we could be seen going over there hand in hand."

"Okay," Jill nodded. "I can do that."

"It's a standing date then," Charming nodded. "Thank you so much for doing this, Jill."

Jill nodded. "No problem."

She was the girl who volunteered to do things even to her detriment, a people pleaser to the end.

She would have to brush off her acting skills now, though.

"Welcome to the family, Jill," Noel shook her hand vigorously.

"We should have dinner soon at the house," Jane said sympathetically.

She looked at Jill with such pity. She probably thought that Jill could have only gotten a man like Rodney Charming because his back was against the wall, and he had no other choice.

Jill sighed. She wouldn't let her dark imaginings take her over. They should be happy that she had bought their family member some time for him to sort out his issues.

She was the benevolent one here. They should be glad that she was a chronic people-pleaser.

"Okay, bye, everybody. See you on Sunday, Rodney. See you tomorrow night for the potluck committee, Jane, and see you on Friday night for the finance committee meeting Noel. I have to go to work. I am filling in for the delivery guy today."

They nodded.

She exited the churchyard, pleased that she had done a good deed today.

And she was in excellent spirits until she saw Larry drive by in his new car with Piper at the front.

He slowed down when he saw her exiting the church, but he just tooted his horn and gave her a little wave.

Piper hung through the window and waved at her too.

Jill gritted her teeth. Piper Miller. Interior Designer. Why was she even in Crimson Hills? Why had she grown up to be so gorgeous and friendly? The sight of her yesterday had driven her to eat six chocolate-coated, cream-filled donuts.

Piper was a reminder of a really low time in her life. And now, to add fuel to the fire, she was also working with Larry, and that made Jill as jealous as ever.

She was steaming with it. If she didn't have some deliveries to do this morning, she would eat a tub of ice cream to help with her stomach burn and jealousy. Everybody knew that ice cream fixed jealousy and stomach burn.

****

"I can't believe you went through with it," Larry looked at Jill's ring hand incredulously. "The ring isn't even on the right finger!"

She had just locked up the store and was heading toward the potting shed to feed her feline friends and inform them of her new status.

"Larry, how pleasant to see you," Jill said sweetly. "And for your information, we did not exchange rings. This is my regular jewelry."

"Let me make a wild guess," Larry said. "He told you his sob story. You agreed to marry him anyway, and he pushed the date up in case you changed your mind. He is slick. I have to give him that."

"Why do you care?" Jill asked, opening the side gate. "You looked quite chummy with Piper today. By the way, you two look good together."

"She's a co-worker, nothing more," Larry said. "I hope you seeing her with me didn't trigger this mad dash to the altar with Charming."

"You have always thought too highly of yourself," Jill said. "There was no mad dash to the altar. I am helping Rodney out."

"I can't believe this," Larry husked. "How am I supposed to deal with the fact that you are a married woman?"

"I didn't know that my marriage would affect you so deeply," Jill looked at him, shocked. "Are you playing around again?"

"No," Larry growled. "I don't play around with you. I have always been serious, but none of that matters now that you are married. I don't mess with married women; you made a commitment to another man. I can't believe this."

He really was devastated. Jill swallowed. What if she had made a mistake, and this was not how her life was supposed to be?

What if she never developed an affection for Rodney? What if she would always be attracted to Larry? She would be married to one man while yearning for another.

She headed to the potting shed. Her gang of twelve was waiting for her. They greeted her vocally as usual.

"Do you still sit and talk to them like they can understand you?" Larry asked.

Jill looked around. "I didn't realize that you followed me."

"I thought I would hang out with you since I cleared my evening," Larry said, "at least you'll have a human to talk to and not these lot. I can't believe Brownie and Marms are still here."

Marms looked over at him when she heard her name and came to give him a thorough sniff.

"You are looking as young and sweet as ever," he stooped down, and she rubbed herself on him, Larry caressed her, and she started purring.

Some of the cats walked over to him to get some of the treatment that Marms was getting, and Larry obliged, trying to touch as many of them as he could.

Larry chuckled. "When I came back a year ago, I was going to get a cat or two, but mom and dad already had Marassa and Midnight. And they've been gravitating to my house more these days."

"I don't understand it. Why do they love you so much?" Jill headed to the cupboard for the food. The cats quickly forgot about Larry and started vocalizing their encouragement for her to hurry.

Larry laughed. "I am quiet and relaxed; I allow them to dictate their own terms in a relationship with me. I don't chase them for affection. Chasing them doesn't work. It makes them skittish. I allow them to come to me, they view me as non-threatening, and then they demand the petting and cuddling."

"Oh really, so that's how it works?" Jill chuckled.

"It worked with you before," Larry sat down in one of the rocking chairs. "Unfortunately, it didn't work this time around. I waited too long for you to come to your senses, and now you are tied up with Charming."

"He told me his story," Jill said, "it has a ring of truth to it. And it was no skin off my back to help him out."

"So, what's the game plan?" Larry said after she fed the cats. "How are you going to navigate this 'marriage'?"

"I'll lose the weight and then have a proper ceremony," Jill sat in the chair across from Larry.

"So until then, you are just going to be living in limbo?" Larry asked, confused. "You'll be Mrs. Charming, but not really?"

"Something like that," Jill swallowed, "Lee said losing a hundred pounds was doable."

"I guess it is doable for the women who don't own a bakery or emotionally eat," Larry murmured. "But you have all the cookies and cakes and donuts and pies at your fingertips, and you load up when stressed."

"I'll need to find a better way to handle my stress." Jill started rocking in the chair. "The truth is, I can't be eating as I have been, at this point I am just playing with fire. And by fire I mean all sorts of lifestyle diseases. Any way you look at this, marrying Rodney has been a blessing."

"Come on, Jill," Larry snorted. "You didn't have to marry the man to lose weight. I offered to help you; we could do it together. I gave you an excuse for us to spend more time with each other, and you blew it. None of your gossipy church sisters would find it odd that you are walking up and down the hills with me or working out at my house.

"They'd wonder, but they wouldn't get their tongues wagging. And then, after a time appropriate to you, we'd get married and have little Lills and Jarrys running around the place. I would even occasionally come to your church, even though you know I am highly against organized religion."

"We are unequally yoked," Jill said.

"I disagree," Larry shrugged, "and that's your grandmother talking. We both believe in God, don't we?"

Jill nodded.

"We both like right doing, but I can sniff out a scam a mile away, and you, unfortunately, will fall for any sob story."

Jill laughed. "I am getting wiser."

"Not really. You married Rodney Charming." Larry sighed. "He read you right. He came to you with a story that would pull on your heartstrings, he supposedly spilled all his deep dark secrets, maybe even shed a tear or two and you fell for it, hook, line and sinker. Your problem is you are too nice."

Jill squeezed her eyes shut and sighed. "I am too nice."

"I wouldn't have required any of the nonsense he did in order to marry you," Larry whispered. "If today was our wedding day, we would be in bed right now. We probably would stay there for a full week. I have a lot of years to make up for with you."

Jill opened her eyes. "Larry!"

Larry chuckled. "Stop acting so brand-new, Jill. I have always wanted you, and I don't care about your size."

"Why are you so basic?" Jill growled. "And why is it always about sex with you?"

"I am a man; you are the woman I desire, and I must confess it gives me a certain joy to tease you about sex because you are so uptight about it." Larry shrugged. "What made you so uncomfortable with your sexuality? You used to be so different."

"I was slimmer then," Jill growled, "and I wasn't as serious about my faith. I went through a little rebellion phase."

"Ah," Larry nodded. "So your excuse is that you are too fat now and bound by church rules?"

"Yes," Jill hissed, "and there is nothing wrong with that."

"I think there is something wrong with your outlook." Larry shrugged, "your insecurities and preconceived beliefs made you throw away your life on a man who doesn't want you unless you are slimmer. And yet, here I am, a man who wants you whatever size you are, and you keep pushing me away.

"As far as I see right now, there are two options before you, marriage less sex, or sex without marriage, and you chose the marriage less sex. What will you do when your healthy sexual urges chip in."

"Stop talking," Jill murmured. Marms jumped into her lap, and Brownie quickly followed.

"I would offer to help you," Larry said, "but unfortunately, I have this rule about sleeping with married women."

"Just get out, Larry," Jill said tiredly. "Nobody is going to commit adultery. I am fine. I will be fine. I'll lose the weight and have a normal marriage, you'll see."

Larry nodded. "As much as I hate that your end goal to losing weight is having sex with Charming, a piece of me wants you to lose the weight so that you can hopefully have a healthier view of yourself. You are a beautiful woman, and I would love for you to see what I see."

Jill looked over at him. "You'd really help me, despite the fact that I would be losing weight to be with someone else?"

"Yep, why not?" Larry nodded. "I have a feeling as you shed the weight and get to love yourself, even more, a bit of that people-pleasing will end. A little self-preservation never hurt anybody. By the end of this, you'll be ditching Rodney Charming and begging me to pet you instead. And I will, I'll make you purr…."

"Larry," Jill said weakly.

"I was just using the cat imagery," he said, stroking Oreo, who had jumped in his lap and was purring loudly. His phone pinged with a message, and he checked it.

"Unfortunately, I am going to have to leave you soon."

"Why? Hot date?" Jill asked jealously.

"Nope. I have to babysit. My mom is working late tonight, and the babysitter needs to be relieved."

"Shay and Jeremiah are off on honeymoon?" Jill asked.

"Yep," Larry nodded, "and the family is in charge of Cerise until then."

"I heard that Shay is pregnant," Jill said wistfully, "and she didn't have to do IVF this time."

"That's right, a true miracle." Larry winked at her. "One you'll probably never experience with this piecemeal marriage of yours."

Jill swallowed.

"I have to go. Miss Oakley deserves a break, and I want some uncle time with Cerise before she falls asleep. She truly is an outstanding conversationalist."

Jill chuckled. "That baby is not talking yet."

"Well, not clearly," Larry shrugged, "she's just like your cats. A meow here and there lets you know where her headspace is at."

Jill hooted with laughter, alarming her kitties, and the two in her lap jumped off.

She followed Larry to the door. "I had quite forgotten the fun I used to have with you."

"When you go to bed tonight, remember how it was and what we lost by you marrying this guy."

He kissed her swift and hard. But it was enough to make her weak.

"Goodbye, Mrs. Charming," Larry said, "sweet dreams."

Jill couldn't speak. She just nodded. She watched Larry's retreating back.

When she couldn't see him anymore, she went right back to her armchair, she was going to do what he said and think about them. Think about the summer when she had discovered what it was to be his girlfriend.

Chapter Eleven

Summer Seven Years Ago

"Is your grandmother around?" Someone asked above her head. Jill was just about to remove the last piece of cake from the display and have a go at it. It was her birthday, and she had told her grandmother not to bake her a cake. She was on a diet again. This diet wasn't even hard. When she was hungry, she drank coconut water. For twenty-one days, she was on it, and she had lost twenty pounds. She couldn't remember feeling so slim and free.

With a heavy heart, she took the perfect slice of cake out of the display case and stood up with the temptation in her hand.

"You didn't answer." Larry Nelson grinned. "What's going on with you, Jill?"

Jill gasped. He knew her name. Larry Nelson, the town bad boy rebel, knew her name. He leaned casually on the case and looked at her wickedly.

"She er…" Jill cleared her throat. "She is gone to a church convention at one of our sister churches in Falmouth. Can I help you with something?"

He grinned broadly, the dimples at the side of his mouth deepened. He looked at her and slowly ran his tongue over his lips. "Well, you could…."

He left his sentence hanging in the air while he looked her up and down. "You could go out with me tonight since she is not here."

"I…I what are you talking about?" Jill asked, flustered. Larry had never paid her any attention before. He rode up and down the hill with his bike like a demented bat out of hell. When he was driving his father's car, he turned the music up so loud you knew when he was passing by, and usually, he played the most inappropriate songs. And if that wasn't bad enough, he was banned from church because he would stand up and correct the pastor in mid-sermon and disrupt the church proceedings.

He was cute, though. Really cute. The kind of cute that would burst into seriously handsome the older he got. He was just eighteen. She shouldn't be thinking about how cute he was. She was twenty-one, an adult woman who should have more of a mature taste.

"We could buy some food?" Larry said, "Then go up to Crimson Hill Great House to eat. You can carry that cake with you."

"I am not supposed to be eating," Jill said stoutly. "I am on a diet. I haven't eaten anything for twenty-one days. If I eat now, I will probably do more harm to my stomach than good."

Larry laughed. "That's why you were looking at that piece of cake like it was the best thing you had ever seen."

Jill smiled shyly. "I was trying to justify eating it. Today is my birthday. I have nine days of this fast to go, and I hope to lose thirty pounds. I would be in my one nineties for the first time in years."

"We can't let your birthday go by without celebrating," Larry said, "and I am no nutritionist, but people who do crash diets like that usually put back on all the weight they lose plus more."

"I won't," Jill shrugged. "This time, I'll eat right for every meal. I'll just treat food like fuel."

"That's boring," Larry said, "life is so much better when you eat for flavor and taste, when every bite of food is an adventure."

"I can't do that," Jill shrugged. "If I just look at food, I put on weight."

"Technically, that's impossible," Larry smirked. "Your problem is you treat food like a reward and punishment. Maybe it was taught to you, or maybe you started the unhealthy practice on your own, but when you starve yourself for thirty days as a weight loss tool, trust me, when you start eating again, it will be epic. You'll think, I lost thirty pounds, so surely I can have this or that, and before you know it, by the end of the week you'll regain all the weight."

Jill glared at him; this was not her first rodeo with a crash diet. She usually put the weight back on within a week or two. Larry may be a rebel, but he was pretty wise for his age.

"So, what do you expect me to do," Jill asked. "Just break my diet?"

"Yes, celebrate your birthday," Larry winked. "You only live once, eat all the foods, drink all the wine. Well, not wine. Maybe that would make you sick. I'll drink it for you. By the way, how old are you?"

"Twenty-one," Jill said. "I shouldn't be hanging with you, Larry. My grandmother would kill me if she found out. Besides, you are too young and too infamous."

Larry laughed. "Your grandmother would never kill her favorite grandchild. Besides, some of my infamy is pure rumors and speculation. You should get to know me and see if they are true."

"I don't know," Jill dithered.

"It's just for the summer," Larry said, "I'll be leaving for university soon."

"You got into university?" Jill asked, shocked.

Larry laughed. "Oh, my ego. Yes, I did. I got in last year. I took a gap year."

"Where?" Jill asked, disbelief rife in her voice. Larry was the last person she thought of going to college. He just didn't strike her as someone who took life seriously.

"Georgia Tech. Civil Engineering." Larry shrugged, "I may do an associate in interior design too."

"Oh wow," Jill widened her eyes. "I always thought you were a…a…."

"Troublemaker without any sense." Larry finished for her. "I know your grandmother certainly thinks so. I challenge her quite a bit about some Bible concepts. She doesn't like the challenge."

Jill grinned. "So what do you want her for?"

"I don't." Larry shrugged. "I saw her on the church bus heading away, and I came here to see if you were free to hang with me."

"Me?" Jill squealed, "I didn't know you knew I existed."

"Of course, I know you exist." Larry grinned. "I've had a crush on you since high school. You didn't notice me then, but I had an eye on you. I also knew it was your birthday. I know a lot of things about you, Jill."

Jill giggled nervously. No one had ever had a crush on her before. Especially someone who looked like Larry Nelson. It was heady business. She needed to sit down before she fainted from excitement.

"I should go wrap this up," she mumbled.

"And take it with you," Larry said, "at least you can have soup or something. We can eat at a restaurant in Falmouth."

"I don't think…" she bit her lip before she said anything else. Why shouldn't she enjoy herself? It was her birthday. Her other options were going upstairs to the apartment alone, reading a novel, and drinking boring coconut water. If she were to be honest, it was beginning to taste awful.

"Okay," Jill nodded, "but nobody can know about us hanging out."

Larry smiled. "That's fine, our secret."

****

They had been practically inseparable since then. They always met up at Crimson Hill Great House or her grandmother's potting shed when Sally Wimple wasn't around. Jill had taken to curling up in there and reading, so her grandmother had not found it strange when she hung out up there all hours of the night after they closed the bakery.

Jill had been fascinated with Larry. He had a sharp wit and intelligence that belied his age and was equally fascinated with her.

"I don't like your bike," she told him one night. It was raining outside. They were sitting close together on her grandmother's shaggy brown rug and leaning on the old sofa. A few cats were on the sofa, and a few at their feet. They had only six cats at the time.

"Okay, I'll stop riding it," Larry murmured. "I have been

thinking of selling it anyway."

"Just like that?" Jill asked.

"Just like that." Larry took her hand in his. "I feel as if I would do anything for you."

"We've only been seeing each other for four weeks," Jill curled her fingers around his, "and you are going off to university. This is not permanent; it's a summer fling. A secret summer fling."

"Emphasis on secret," Larry chuckled. "What else about me you don't like?"

"Well, I don't like the fact that you smoke. I think it's a terrible habit."

"Okay," Larry nodded. "I'll quit."

Jill chuckled. "Now I know you are joking; people go to rehab to quit smoking."

"Not everyone," Larry chuckled. "People quit on their own every day; it may be hard at first, I have been smoking for four years, but I can give it up."

"Why did you start?" Jill asked.

"I was bored." Larry shrugged. "I saw some guys smoking at a construction site we were working at, and I asked them if I could try. When I did, I realized that I felt stronger, the colors were brighter, and whenever I wanted to vent about something my mom or dad did, just a few inhales, made me mellow. I started smoking if I was sad, smoking if I was glad. I used it as a crutch for my emotions."

"Like I do with eating?" Jill whispered.

"I guess so." Larry looked at her, "I figure my addiction will be much easier to overcome than yours."

"How do you figure?" Jill frowned.

"Well, you work at a bakery," Larry said, "you work with the things that tempt you."

"That's true. I wonder why I am the only one with this

problem. I can't see a cake and not want to eat it," Jill said. "Do you know that my grandmother is the weight she was when she just got married? And she has been working in a bakery since she was sixteen!"

"Goodness," Larry gasped, "for the past hundred years!"

"Grandma is in her sixties," Jill chuckled. "I wish you would get to know her. You would like her."

"She thinks I am lower than the dirt under her shoe," Larry smirked. "She thinks I am the antichrist."

"Maybe you shouldn't argue with her about the Bible," Jill said, "she has a simple faith; she doesn't like being challenged on the things you challenge her on. She doesn't know about the history of the book, she doesn't know about other religions, and she has no idea about Jesus' real name. She doesn't know any of that, and she doesn't care. She grew up with a certain worldview, and she has lived like that all her life, and that's the way she likes it."

"I can't help myself," Larry shrugged, "I think most religions place God in a little bottle, they fashion him and make him to suit their philosophy, and then they look down on you when you don't agree with them."

Jill nodded. "I understand what you are saying. You are a seeker. You thirst for knowledge, you ask questions, and the answers have to make sense; if not, you get frustrated. That's where you and Grandma are similar; both of you stubbornly wish that the other would see things your way."

"You know me." Larry looked at her wonderingly. "You really do. I have never been able to put into words what you just described about me and religion."

"I know you because I was like that too, not outwardly like you. I didn't have the balls to question things outright like that. I admire how you just ask questions and put yourself out there." Jill sighed. "I find it easier to conform and make peace with what I've have been brought up with. Life is much easier that way. Even if the explanations don't make sense. I just have faith that at the end of the day, if you do the right by others and the community around you, then that should count for something."

"I'll never conform." Larry shrugged, "conformers don't learn new things. Conformers don't expand and grow."

"I know," Jill nodded, "but some people just want to get on with the daily grind. They don't want to rock the boat. They want to fit in with their community and society, and questioning things too much will unmoor them to what they consider safe. I am one of those people."

"I have to find a way to make you not be such a conformist," Larry grinned.

"And I guess I have to find a way to make you a little more diplomatic and accepting of the conformists," Jill smirked.

"Okay then, it's a deal," Larry leaned toward her, "let's kiss to seal it."

"I have never kissed anyone before," Jill said, "my grandma said that kissing is a gateway to…."

She never finished her speech; Larry placed his lips over hers. It was electrifying. They kissed so long that they had to both come up for air.

"Wow," Jill said, touching her lips.

****

The telephone jerked Jill out of her trip down memory lane. It was Rodney.

He sounded quite panicky. "Er… Jill. Just a heads up, my aunt Jane told her friends that we got married this morning. She is also throwing a dinner party at the manse after church this Sunday to celebrate our marriage."

Jill groaned. "Why didn't you stop her?"

"I couldn't. My uncle Noel was the one who suggested it. He wanted the elders to be a part of it, so our secret is out. He says he wants this marriage as public as possible. Everyone is invited after church."

Jill groaned. "Well, you married me so they would know you are no longer single."

"That's true," Rodney said. "By the way, I told my uncle that you agreed to marry me now, but our marriage will not be exactly watertight until you lose a hundred pounds. He thinks it's a great idea."

"He does?" Jill coughed.

"When I think about it, it's not exactly a bad idea if everyone knows," Rodney said.

"No," Jill got up from the armchair and headed to the door. "I don't want everybody to know I am trying to lose weight to have a normal marriage. You know what, when I get off the phone with you, I will get the ball rolling."

"You are?" Rodney sounded surprised.

"Yup," Jill closed the door and ensured the cat flap was opened. "I will call Lee and tell him I am ready to begin."

"I thought Lee was not going to be around," Rodney's voice didn't sound as upbeat as before, Jill noted, but she didn't care.

"Larry said he would help in his absence," Jill said, "he has a gym at his house too."

"Okay, go at it," Rodney said weakly.

Jill called Lee as soon as she reached the apartment.

"Come on over Saturday night," Lee answered. He was still in the gym; she could hear the music and background noises on his end. "And take Larry with you. If he is going to stand in for me, he needs to be up to speed. Oh, and make a record of everything you have eaten for the past two weeks and make a note of the times and email it to me before Saturday night. Be as honest as possible."

"Sure thing," Jill said and hung up.

Chapter Twelve

Larry had one of those restless nights where he couldn't sleep. He was more disturbed about Jill getting married than he had initially thought. It had been on his mind so much he had retreated to his home gym, where he had proceeded to beat up his punching bag. His arms were hurting him rather intensely that morning. He shouldn't have overdone it.

He walked into his parents' kitchen for breakfast. As usual, there was a spread laid out buffet style because his parents had a full-time cook. None of them bothered to cook at home if they could help it and Bobby and Bunny usually welcomed the company for breakfast.

Mercedes, Rory, and his dad were already eating. All of them were scrolling through their devices. His mom was the only exception; she was feeding Cerise. His little niece was dressed in a romper that said I love my uncle Larry.

He looked at it and chuckled. He had gotten quite a few of them done in varying colors and sizes for her.

"Good morning, everyone," he said less than brightly.

His father looked up from his iPad, registering his voice. "Why so glum?"

Mercedes and Rory both looked at him too curiously.

"Jill got married to Pastor Charming," Bunny answered. "Yesterday morning in a secret ceremony, I expected Larry to be grim this morning."

"I am feeling a little heart sore and hand sore, to be honest. I spent the night beating up my punching bag. But I'll live," Larry said morosely. "I don't even have an appetite."

He poured himself some ginger tea. "I should go. I have a virtual meeting with Mr. Hendrickson. And then, I have a site visit at Edgar Green's place in Cascade Hills. Is anybody available to work on Edgar Green's plans?"

"Nobody," Bobby said, "it's all hands on deck at the Pleasant Hill project right now."

"When is Jeremiah coming back?" Larry asked.

"Sunday evening," Bunny said. "You may have to do the drawings yourself."

"Okay," Larry muttered, "until then, I'll have to go to that meeting and then tackle Cascade Hills."

Mercedes cleared her throat. "Jill got married?"

Larry sighed. "Yes."

"Do you want to talk to me about it? I have ten minutes. And then we can schedule something tonight."

Larry grimaced. "No, I am fine."

"You are clearly not fine," Mercedes said. "You think immersing yourself in work will help, but I doubt it will; it will just delay your reactions. You may blow up at someone at work today."

"They would deserve it," Larry said.

"Wait a minute," Bunny said, concerned. "I said I was going to stay out of this, but you can't go blowing up at anyone. You have to remain professional. If you think you need the day, take it."

"I don't need the day," Larry said, "I will be fine."

"You should have married her seven years ago and locked her down," Rory said helpfully.

Larry glared at his little brother. He probably would have married Jill if he had the chance; he had known even back then she was the woman he had always wanted to be with. The thought irked him that Jill would not have said yes to a proposal. He had been her secret; she was afraid to tell her parents or grandmother about seeing him.

He snapped at Rory because he was spurned, and that was not an option. "Just because you got married when you were a baby doesn't mean everybody has to."

"I know that's right," Bunny mumbled.

"What are you doing here anyway? And where is your wife?" Larry asked snidely.

Rory grinned, unperturbed by his waspishness. "I live here, and my wife is staying with her mother."

"At the go-go club," Bunny said helpfully.

Larry chuckled. "She is not dancing, is she?"

"No," Rory said calmly, "we have a wedding to attend later. So, we came down from school for it. Jewel is a bridesmaid."

"Ah," Larry nodded. "All I hear about these days are weddings."

"And birthdays," Bunny grinned. "Are you sure you don't want me to have a big party for your birthday?"

"Positive," Larry nodded. "I don't have anything to celebrate."

"Well then, I am just going to have to plan for Cerise's birthday party. It will be in four months. My gorgeous little cherry plum is going to be one," Bunny cooed to the baby.

"I can't believe it. Time flies, but I love it. I love watching her grow up."

She was a pretty baby, Larry thought fondly; she looked like a feminine version of Jeremiah. And Jeremiah looked a lot like Bunny. Cerise was going to be spoiled rotten as Bunny's grandchild.

"You and Jill would have pretty babies, too," Bunny said, looking at him knowingly. "But that's all water under the bridge now, isn't it? She is married to another man, and you are alone and single."

"Mom!" Mercedes protested, "that was an unnecessarily cruel thing to say."

Larry sighed. "I know how cruel mom can be to little old me."

"I wasn't cruel," Bunny said, "I was just stating a fact. It would have been cruel of me to tell you that Jane White is inviting the whole family to an after-church dinner to celebrate the nuptials of Pastor and Mrs. Charming this Sunday after church, but I didn't tell you that did I?"

Larry got up. "I have to go."

"Are you going to be okay, Larry?" Bobby asked, concerned.

"Yes," Larry nodded. "It's just another day."

His father did not accept that. He still looked worried. He was the only one who understood the state he had been in when Jill rejected their relationship seven years ago. He had dropped him at the airport for school and had ended up buying a ticket and going with him to Georgia to make sure he was okay.

Larry double-checked himself. Today felt the same as if a piece of him had shriveled up and died. It was the hopeful part of him, he thought inanely. The part of him that still clung to some sort of happily ever after with Jill. The part of him that knew it was over for good.

He got in the car, plugged his phone into the car's audio, and turned on a playlist to drown out his thoughts.

Unfortunately, it was the playlist he had entitled Jill, and the first song on it was: If You're Not the One by Daniel Bedingfield.

That song always reminded him of the first time they had made love and the last night before he left Jamaica.

If I'm not made for you, then why does my heart tell me that I am?

That line of the song packed a punch. Larry almost stopped the car and pulled over so the tightness in his chest could ease. Why was he acting this way? He had a whole year to convince Jill to have a relationship with him, he had given her time, and the time had run out. He felt like it was a kind of death. She could no longer be his in his head. Well, only in his memories…

****

Seven Years Ago

"I leave for school in a week," Larry said. "I wish I didn't have to leave you."

Jill looked over at him wordlessly. She was driving her grandmother's delivery van and concentrating hard on the road. The visibility was getting poorer by the minute as angry clouds rolled over the horizon.

"You have to go," Jill said, "these are the years when you find yourself, when you discover who you really are."

"I think I have discovered who I am this summer," Larry said, "I kicked the smoking habit and stopped swearing."

"As much," Jill snorted.

"As much," Larry nodded, "And I discovered that I love a girl named Jillian Wimple."

Jill slowed down, reached across, and kissed him, "I love you too, Larry."

"But you still want me to leave?" Larry pressed, "I could stay and go to school out here so I can be with you every day."

"No," Jill said firmly. "You are still so young; what you want at eighteen is not what you are going to want at twenty-one. Trust me, on this, I am not the same girl I was a few short years ago. We become a whole different person every couple of years. You'll meet friends, lose friends, and lose contact with people you think you can't do without. You'll forget me; you'll move on. It's life and its ebb and flow."

"I'll never forget you," Larry said, "and I'll return as soon as I am done.

As soon as you touch down on campus and you see all the hot girls you'll wonder aloud, what was the name of the fat girl in Jamaica again?"

Larry snorted. "Not happening. I love the fat girl in Jamaica."

"You'll be partying like a madman."

"I'm going to live in my Aunt Wendy's basement apartment." Larry grinned. "No parties. Besides, I hate parties."

"You'll change your mind." Jill chuckled. "And with your personality and looks, you'll have people flocking to you in no time. Just remember to balance that and schoolwork. Remember your dreams. You're going to conquer the construction world with eco-friendly buildings."

Larry chuckled softly. "You sound like my career counselor. I didn't say I am going to conquer. I would say I'm going to help in the family business and make some waves.”

He frowned because the place had progressively started to get darker. Jill had to turn on her headlights though it was just four o'clock in the evening. The sun didn't set until nearly seven, so this was worrying.

They were in the Cascade Hills, his mother's hometown. Cascade Hills was almost an hour from Crimson Hills. Jill had made a late delivery because the van was at the mechanic for most of the day.

It was good that he had seen her driving out and decided to come along for the ride because he didn't think he would want her out here alone in this type of weather on Cascade Hills' narrow roads.

“We had better stop,” Larry said, looking through the window. “It's not safe to drive over the bridge at the bottom of this road. It’s usually flooded when there are heavy rains.”

“We can't stop,” Jill said. “Where would we stop? I need to get to the bridge before it starts raining.”

“That's not going to happen,” Larry said when the first sounds of rain started pelting the van. “Luckily, my grandparents live near here, Larry said. And Mom and Dad have a cottage. I know where the keys are kept.”

“Look at this rain?” Jill groaned. She slowed to a crawl. “How far away are your grandparents?”

“My grandparents are about four minutes around the corner, I think.” The visibility was so poor. He couldn’t really see outside.

“I am scared,” Jill looked at him wide-eyed, “I have this fear that I would drive over one of the cliffs.”

“Relax,” Larry said soothingly, “the cliffs are on that side of the road.”

“Why are you so calm?” Jill asked. “You look like you are loving this.”

"I just love hanging with you," Larry smiled. "It feels like we are the only two people in the world. Surrounded by a waterfall."

Jill grimaced. "I will romanticize this when we are parked and out of this rain."

"Rain music," Larry said, distracting her. "What's your favorite rain song?"

"You mean a song with rain in it?" Jill asked, "I don't think my windshield wipers are doing anything in this deluge. I can't see an inch in front of me."

"I don't know that song," Larry mused.

"You are funny," Jill smirked, "my song is Umbrella by Rihanna. I used to sing that song at the top of my voice when it just came out. I was about twelve."

Larry started humming it, When the sun shines, we'll shine together, told you I'll be here forever, said I'll always be your friend…you can stand under my umbrella…

"You have a nice voice," Jill grinned at him.

"Thank you," Larry said wryly, "for a brief period in my childhood, Bunny had Mercedes and me singing together at church and for family functions."

"Is there any video?" Jill chuckled.

"Of course," Larry sighed, "loads and loads of it. When we get to the cottage, there are tons of family footage, with us as children doing all sorts of things, singing, and skits and birthday parties."

"I want to see it," Jill grinned, "what's your rain song?"

"Here Comes the Rain Again," Larry grinned, "by the Eurythmics."

"I don't know it," Jill frowned, "what does it say?"

"Are you serious?" Larry grinned, "for someone who is always emphasizing our age difference, you should know this, Jill. It's an eighties song."

"I am a nineties baby." Jill grinned. "Sing one line."

Here comes the rain again, falling on my head like a memory… talk to me like lovers do…

"I know it," Jill said. "I haven't heard that song in ages. It made me feel like dancing in the rain."

"Dancing in the rain, huh?" Larry chuckled, "have you ever done that?"

"No," Jill said, "I might look ridiculous, so I haven't tried it."

"That's no reason not to do something, dance like no one is looking. You only live once. Take advantage of this gift."

"Is that why you used to race up and down the hill like a lunatic on your bike?" Jill asked.

"There is nothing like it." Larry laughed, "But that is tame compared to the things I have done in my day. I lost a bet with my brothers, and I had to walk naked from our home to Crimson Hill Great House."

"That's not true." Jill gasped.

"Yup," Larry nodded, "Jeremiah and Rory can attest to the fact that they were grinning all the way behind me to ensure I did it."

"What did your parents do?"

"They found out long after when somebody mentioned it to Bunny; she was mortified." Larry laughed. "She threatened to lock us up in the house because we are an embarrassment."

Jill laughed.

"Turn right here," Larry pointed to the Cascade Hills Drive sign. It seemed like it came out of nowhere in the van's floodlights.

"My grandparents are in the cul de sac, at the end of the road. Keep on driving," Larry said.

Jill whistled. "I didn't know this community existed. I am

looking forward to seeing the houses when the rain eases up. They look like they could be nice."

Larry chuckled. "They are. From the top of the road to the end, all this land belonged to my grandfather. Forty acres of land. He gave each of his ten children two acres and sold the other twenty in one-acre slots. Most of the houses here are new buildings. I can recall coming up here at eight, and there was nothing around but cows in the distance and a few spots here and there where people used to farm."

"I didn't know your grandfather was rich. Bunny said she grew up poor."

"I guess it probably seemed like that to her. After all, unimproved land doesn't equal spending money," Larry said. "Grandpa was a farmer; grandma sold his goods in the Falmouth market. They had ten children, so resources were spread thin. They didn't start selling off the land until their children were adults. The land had been in the family for ages."

"Slow down. This is it." Larry murmured. Lights were on in the two-story cottage-style house. "We drive through the main gates. The road beside it leads to our cottage."

The rain had let up some, and things were more visible.

"This is cleverly done," Jill said, "there is one main gate, and then you have a house at the front, but when you drive around, another house appears with its own lawn and fences. She stopped in the cobblestone driveway. Where does the road lead to?"

"Uncle Al's place," Larry said. "This is the same setup we will have at Crimson Hills, you know. There will be a whole community behind the main house. Dad gave each of us a quarter acre to design and build our own house."

Jill nodded. "You must do something good, at least three bedrooms, a gym, and a sauna."

Larry nodded. "Okay."

"I am joking," Jill said, "don't let me dictate to you what to build."

"Why not?" Larry smiled, "you'll probably be living in it with me."

"Shouldn't you tell your grandparents that we are here?" Jill changed the subject abruptly and tried to look past the thick hedge that separated the houses.

"They probably don't know we are here," Larry said, "if the rain eases, I'll say something, but they are used to traffic going by their house. My uncle lives behind our cottage with his family."

Larry peered out the windshield and looked at the place proudly. "This was the very first place I had ever contributed to building. It was the first time that I realized just what my father did, and I wanted to be just like him when he grew up.

"It is a simple three-bedroom bungalow style place, but it brings to mind summers of fun; being carefree and happy, playing with my siblings and cousins, and barbecues in the backyard."

Jill cleared her throat, "this house is not a cottage. It's a mini-mansion."

Larry laughed. "It's just a three-bedroom, two-bathroom place. My dad built it so that we wouldn't have to sleep in the main house when we stayed over and that there would be room for spillovers from the main house when we weren't around. My mom's family is large, and there is an unspoken rule that everybody gathers here for the summer."

"It's still summer," Jill said, "is anyone in there?"

"Nope," Larry said, "Aunt Linda and her brood left two days ago. They stayed here. Aunt Kay and Marie are still over at grandma and granddad. I will get out, deactivate the alarm, find an umbrella, and come back for you."

He raced to open the door, but he couldn't find an umbrella to go for Jill.

He darted back to the van, "You will have to make a dash for it."

Jill opened the door, but in the haste to get out of the rain her bag strap got stuck between the hand brake and her seat. By the time she wrestled it free and joined Larry on the veranda, they were both soaking wet.

She smiled at him.

"You are so pretty," Larry said.

Jill smiled wider. "Thank you, kind sir."

"You are also wet," Larry said.

"So are you." Jill looked behind her at the pouring rain. "It didn't feel bad at all."

"We are soaking wet already; we should just take a bath out here," Larry said jokingly.

"Okay, let's do it," Jill said.

"Are you serious?" Larry was surprised.

"Yup, didn't you just say we only live once," Jill said, "let's go back out. You have a washing machine and dryer inside, don't you?"

Larry nodded.

"Let's get soaked." Jill ran back out in the front yard with her arms spread wide. "It's not bad at all, Larry. I've always wanted to do this."

Larry joined her, laughing. "I am going to strip down to my underwear."

"I am going to strip down to my shapewear," Jill said giddily.

Larry laughed. He had never seen Jill like this before, completely uninhabited, and clearly thrilled to be out in the driving rain.

They took off their clothes and hopped around in the rain

singing rain songs.

****

"How long do you think this rain will go on?" Jill asked after they had run inside and showered.

Their clothes were chugging along in the dryer, but Larry had found a pair of jeans and t-shirt, and a robe that could fit Jill from the third bedroom, where his various relatives left their odds and ends. The housekeeper who came by after each stay usually washed and hung up the clothes left behind.

"It's not the rain we have to worry about; it's the bridge," Larry said. "After a rain like this, it's basically impassable to vehicular traffic. Bunny said back in her school days, she knew that when it was raining and they left school, they would have to leave the vehicle behind and walk over the bridge. And then she would have the two-mile trek to come up to the house."

"So we may have to spend the night then?"

"Maybe," Larry said, "maybe not. We'll see. We have the time. It's just after five. If we had to sleep over, we have space."

He waved his arms to emphasize the open floor plan space. His father had built it nearly ten years ago. It had been intended to be a spacious and airy, no-frills space. There was a kitchen to the left, a dining room with large windows overlooking the lawn, and a Keit mango tree that had not stopped bearing even though it was the second week of August. The two bedrooms on one side of the house had a shared bathroom, and the other side of the house had a master suite.

Larry used to share with Rory and Jeremiah, and Mercedes

had her own room because she was a girl, but oftentimes, she could be found in their room occupying the empty bunk bed, keeping them up at night with her stories. An avid reader, Mercedes loved sharing what she read with them.

"Are you hungry?" Larry asked; he jumped up from the settee and headed for the kitchen; there is a distinct possibility that there is food in the cupboards. It's summer, and whoever leaves usually restocks when they leave. Aunt Linda is known to restock with delicious things.

"That's thoughtful," Jill said.

Larry nodded. "My mom's family is thoughtful. They are good people."

The cupboards were stocked, and the fridge was loaded with juice and lite beer.

Jill came behind him. "Step aside, Larry, this is my domain."

Larry laughed. "Okay."

Jill opened the freezer and widened her eyes, "there are packs of salmon fillets in there. Oh, my word, do you know how expensive salmon is here in Jamaica?"

Larry grinned. "To be honest, I haven't a clue. Our helper does it sometimes; I love her honey garlic version."

"You are such a privileged child," Jill snorted.

"And you aren't?" Larry asked, "did I miss the piece of your history where you were born in penury and raised in the streets?"

Jill grinned. "I will not argue with you now, Larry. I have salmon fillets in my sight. Let me see what else is around here."

They ended up eating salmon and mashed potatoes, and for dessert, they found several cases of Ferrero Rocher chocolates in the cupboard.

"How is your diet going?" Larry asked after popping the

seventh one in his mouth.

Jill grinned. "This is my fourteenth. I should stop, but there are just so many of them I feel obligated to help. Are you sure whoever left them behind wasn't stocking them for a special occasion?"

"Quite sure," Larry said sleepily.

Jill got up and headed for the pictures on the mantelpiece. "You guys take a family picture every year?"

"Yup. Usually with grandma and grandpa on the front lawn between the white crape myrtle trees every summer."

"I see," Jill murmured. "Like a yearly family reunion."

"Yes," Larry said.

"Your sister Mercedes looks like your grandmother," Jill looked at him curiously, "I thought she was adopted?"

"She was adopted." Larry nodded, "but she is also related to us. My mother's youngest sister Claudia died in childbirth; they thought Mercedes wouldn't have made it too, but she did."

"Ah," Jill nodded, "I always thought she looked a lot like you, and I was confused."

Larry grinned. "People thought we were twins when we were younger. I am just a year older than she is. Which is quite ironic because she acts like the older one. She is bossy."

"And your favorite sibling." Jill grinned. "You two are close."

"We are," Larry said, "but I don't tell her any secrets that I am told I shouldn't tell."

Jill sighed. "So you haven't told her about us?"

"No," Larry said, "I haven't told anyone about us."

"I am going to have to call my grandmother. It's still raining, and I think it's genuinely dark outside now."

Larry looked at the clock. "You may have to sleep over.

Our first sleepover. It should be fun."

Jill glared at him.

"And totally innocent, tell your grandmother there are three bedrooms here, I can behave myself, but all bets are off if you jump me."

Jill laughed, but she did look contemplative, and Larry found that look interesting.

"I'll call her from the room." Jill headed to the bedroom.

He found a stack of home videos in the meantime.

When Jill came back, she was angry.

"My grandmother thinks that she has to dictate my every move. She said if I am going to stay, I should go out in the rain across to your grandparents' house and ask them to put me up for the night. The woman acts as if I am ten. I am twenty-one years old and quite capable of leading my own life and making my own decisions."

"Calm down," Larry urged, "I have music. Let's listen to some."

He turned on the stereo; his aunt or whoever had used it last was listening to the song If You're Not the One.

He left it on low. It did nothing to calm Jill down.

"I just hate that she thinks that I should walk in the rain to a stranger's house just to avoid staying with you." Jill's voice became husky. "I hate feeling as if I have no self-control, don't eat that, Jill, don't eat this, Jill. Stay away from Larry, Jill. You can't voice your opinions because it will offend Jill. Am I supposed to deprive myself of all life's normal experiences because a million people are telling me who to be and how to live?"

Larry shook his head. "You should try to be authentically you."

"Is it anybody's business if I want to be a big fat food-loving single woman having sex with someone I love."

Larry swallowed.

"Say something, Larry," she almost growled it.

This was Jill, as he had never seen her before.

"Don't censor yourself on my behalf." She stared him straight in the eye. "I am on the pill to help with period pain because I have the worst pains in history. I am all yours if you want."

Larry didn't know what had gotten into shy, reserved Jill, who hardly wanted him to touch her breasts when they kissed, but this girl, he was not going to refuse.

I'll never know what the future brings, But I know you're here with me now. That line of the song caught his attention.

"Is this really what you want, Jill? There can't be any regrets after this."

"No regrets," Jill said. "No regrets at all."

Chapter Thirteen

"Your eyes are red," Piper said when Larry walked into the conference room where they were to have the meeting with Hendrickson. "Rough night?"

"Something like that," Larry nodded.

"Me too," Piper said. "My cousin Lailah woke me up in the middle of the night sobbing. She does this a lot, and I don't want to be heartless and tell her to stop. But it's been a year. She needs to move on."

"Some people never move on," Larry murmured. "They may wallow for the rest of their lives."

"I hope that's not the case for her," Piper said feelingly, "I had to listen to every story, every little sweet thing they did together. They had the perfect love story."

"But he was a crook on his way to jail," Larry said, confused. "What's perfect about that?"

"He wasn't a crook. He did what his bosses told him and got caught up in the results," Piper shrugged. "I wouldn't call him a crook."

"Okay," Larry snorted, "maybe I am judging him by the ill will I feel towards his twin brother. Who I feel is shady as hell. Have you met him?"

Piper nodded. "He was the best man at Roderick's and Lailah's wedding. I was the maid of honor. In all honesty, I couldn't tell them apart. It was useful that Rodney dressed a little differently from the groom because I was confused. Listen, they say there are no perfectly identical twins, but Rodney and Roderick were two sides of the same coin, I tell you. Even their voices were the same. Lailah said she could only tell them apart because Roderick did a discrete tattoo on some part of him to make him instantly identifiable to her because she never wanted to confuse them again."

"They looked that alike?" Larry asked.

"Yep." Piper nodded.

"Maybe you should tell Lailah to come out to Jamaica and get a second chance with the remaining twin," Larry said, "after all, he admitted to me that she was the one woman he had ever loved."

"He did?" Piper widened her eyes. "He still carried a torch for Lailah since their university days?"

Larry nodded. "That's what he said."

"You know that does not sound like a bad idea," Piper mused, "Lailah is not doing anything at the moment. She taught at a community college before she became a housewife, but now that her assets are unfrozen and her insurance money is released, she can live off that for the rest of her life. She can travel and have adventures every day. It is a waste for her to be sitting at home moping about Roderick."

"Why mope about Roderick when his identical twin is here," Larry said wickedly. He didn't know what he would accomplish by having Lailah out here. But he knew for sure that it would make Charming very uncomfortable. And there was no harm in putting the cat among the pigeons and seeing what would happen.

Would Rodney be uncomfortable to the point of annulling the marriage to Jill? He didn't know, but he wanted to find out.

He opened his laptop and showed Piper his mockup design. His phone rang, and he saw the number and groaned.

It was his course supervisor for his doctoral thesis. If it was one thing about Dr. Eden, he was a regular caller. He was very interested in Larry's research on net zero energy building in the Caribbean environment.

"Mr. Nelson," Dr. Eden said when he answered, "I have contacted my colleague in Kingston at the University of the West Indies and bragged about the latest findings in your research. His team came up with varying results from yours, and he wants you to collaborate with them for a few weeks."

Larry groaned. "I do have a full-time job."

"I know," Dr. Eden said, "that is why we have technology, Mr. Nelson; we will meet weekly at a time most suitable for you."

"We?" Larry asked.

"I want to sit in," Dr. Eden said, "I am quite interested in this area, as you know."

"I will get back to you," Larry said, "who is the professor with whom I will work?"

"Dr. Phillip Wimple," Dr. Eden gushed, "brilliant guy, he is a savant in mathematics, but he also dabbles in engineering."

Larry hung up the phone after they finished speaking, feeling shocked. He had never met Jill's parents. And this was how he was going to do it?

The irony of the meeting wasn't lost on him. He had initially done his masters because he had been fascinated with sustainable buildings. The company he had joined after graduating had done a lot of emphasis on building with the environment in mind, and he loved it. So naturally, when they offered to send him and two others to university and bonded them for two years, he was fine with it. He liked doing the practical and getting some theory in the interim. At that point, he had given up on dating, so he didn't mind being busy.

After the master's, his course supervisor told him it was only a few credits for the doctorate. He was in a dynamic area of engineering; new and exciting discoveries were around the corner.

He had returned home to make some practical applications in the Caribbean environment. And here he was, about to collaborate with Jill's father for his final thesis.

He swiveled in his chair and waited for Piper to finish looking at the design.

"Wow," she looked at him, "you thought of everything. I know it's our job, but your attention to detail, especially regarding energy saving, is impeccable."

Larry smiled. "Thank you. That's the way the world is heading."

He stopped smiling when Piper started batting her eyes at him and looking at him like he was some sort of genius. He only wanted one woman to look at him that way, and she was married.

Piper cleared her throat and started frowning. "Well then, let's get this meeting started."

****

Larry had just concluded the meeting with Hendrickson

when he saw his sister heading toward his office.

"I am on lunch break," Mercedes said, "I thought you'd need a listening ear."

"You know what I am going to vent about." He opened his office door. "Pretend I vented and just skip to telling me what to do."

Mercedes laughed. "It doesn't work that way."

She walked into the office and sat down opposite his desk. "These are comfy chairs."

"Oh, excuse me," Piper pushed her head through the door. "What time are we visiting Mr. Green?"

"Three o'clock," Larry said, "I sent you the specs for the James project."

"Yes, I'll take a look at it now." Piper smiled at Mercedes. "Oh, hi, I am Piper."

"Mercedes Nelson." Mercedes smiled.

"As in the car?" Piper asked.

"Yes," Mercedes nodded, "my father was the one who named me. However, I must say though that before the luxury car brand, my name was Spanish in origin. It was taken from the Virgin Mary; her Spanish name was Santa Maria de las Mercedes or Our Lady of the Mercies."

"Dad did not know all that," Larry chuckled, "you were named after the car brand."

Mercedes groaned.

Piper laughed. "See you at three, Larry; nice to meet you, Lady of the Mercies."

"I like her," Mercedes said when Piper left the office. "You should give her a chance to get under your skin."

"Nope," Larry grunted. "What I want to do is to get Jill away from Charming."

Mercedes sighed. "There are several reasons why I think Jill is so solidly stuck in your mind. The first thing I can think of is that you had a heightened emotional interlude, and you keep replaying it, thus consolidating it in your mind."

"What?" Larry said, "tell it to me in layman's terms."

"You slept with her. It was good, maybe your first experience. It will always be unparalleled if you don't create other memories to override it."

"So, in other words, have sex with other people?" Larry raised his eyebrows. "I tried that and always felt like I was cheating on her. Unfortunately, she is still stuck in my head. I don't think it's that. I always had a thing for Jill, even in high school."

Mercedes nodded. "I remember."

"Of course, I have never been good enough for her. I am always going to be too young."

"Three years is nothing," Mercedes said.

"Tell that to Jill." Larry snorted, "she also thinks I am too liberal, too opinionated, too non-conformist, and that I can't love her. She thinks that I am faking it or something. So I left her alone for a year to prove that I could wait for her to make up her mind. And what does she do?" Larry exploded. "She went and married a man who is the antithesis of me. He doesn't want her, doesn't love her, and is only using her for his own selfish gain. He told her she had to lose one hundred pounds before he could have sex with her. In what world is he the one she chooses to tie herself to. Why would she choose the opposite of what is good for her?"

"I know," Mercedes said, "it defies logic."

"The man doesn't even have any intention of loving her. He already loves someone else. Bet you the snake oil salesman Charming didn't tell her that. But then again, even if he did, she would still marry him."

Mercedes sighed. "Jill has a lack of self-respect and needs to build it up. I figure she has suffered from childhood trauma, which has colored her decisions throughout her life. She overcompensates by being nice, never saying no, always helpful and kind even if it kills her."

Larry nodded. "So, how can you help her?"

"I'll give her a call. Find out if I can help in any way? And if I do take her on as a patient, I can't discuss what we talk about."

"Didn't expect you to," Larry sat back in his chair, "and thank you."

"Don't anticipate that the end result of Jill having some self-esteem will be that she'll choose you," Mercedes said gently.

"I don't care." Larry shrugged, "I love her. I always have and always will. But even if she chooses someone else, at least it's not someone who is using her."

Chapter Fourteen

"**S**o, how does it feel to be married?" Dacy asked, looking at Jill while she spun in the mirror.

"It feels like a Thursday," Jill muttered.

They were standing among the tracksuits in Cree, Lee, and Craig's sporting goods store.

Dacy had suggested that they shop for Jill's new fitness life.

"I like these tracksuits," Jill said, "they are comfy. I could get used to wearing them every day. I want one in all of the darker colors."

"Don't get too comfy with them at this size," Dacy said, "you want to shed the weight, remember?"

"I do," Jill nodded. "I am determined this time."

"And I'll help from afar," Dacy said. "I'll call you every night."

"Every night." Jill nodded.

"And call me if you feel even a little twinge of a craving."

They moved toward the cash register.

Dacy pushed a trolly with shoes and clothes, and socks.

Jill reached into her bag for her credit card.

"Don't you dare," Dacy said. "I have to get you five years' worth of gifts for all your birthdays I missed while I was in prison."

The cashier widened her eyes.

Jill chuckled. "You really like to shock people, don't you?"

"Sasha is new; she doesn't know my story yet." Dacy smiled. "She'll get up to speed shortly. We also need some protein powder."

Jill frowned. "We do?"

"It will help with your protein uptake and hunger suppression," Dacy said, "and some multivitamins and some protein bars."

"Protein bars?" Jill raised an eyebrow.

"Sugar-free," Dacy said, "in various flavors. Trust me on this, they don't taste like much, but when you have them around, you'll reach for one instead of donuts."

"I can make my own bars," Jill said, "with the protein powder, I just need the other ingredients. I'll do my own flavors."

"Always a baker at heart," Dacy beamed. "I forgot how you liked to experiment. I'll always remember that guinep cake you made when the food and nutrition teacher challenged us to make a cake using an unpopular ingredient."

""Do you think you could recreate these protein bars or improve upon them and take it on Saturday night for taste testing?"

Jill smiled. "It's on."

"Yup," Dacy clapped her hand in glee. "I will text Larry and have him come by as well. I am so happy I get to share this journey with you. I only wish I could be here for your first three months, but it doesn't matter. I'll be here for all the rest of it. And while I am gone, you are in good hands with Larry."

****

"Trelawny is the prettiest parish in Jamaica," Piper gushed. "Every time I leave the major town and venture into the country areas, I find myself saying the same thing."

Larry grunted. He was contemplating the text he read from Dacy before he got in the car. Saturday Night Truth or Dare Games and protein bar taste testing. Come early for the joint weight loss meeting for Jill at six.

He was feeling a little roughed up emotionally. He didn't know if he wanted to go, even though he said he wanted to help. Mercedes was right. What if she lost the weight after his help and slept with Charming anyway. She would have all the right to do that. He was her husband. The thought sickened Larry.

Piper laughed. "You are so talkative. Can I at least have some background on this site visit?"

Larry looked across at her. "Sorry about that. I have a lot on my mind today. Our customer is Edgar Green. He is planning to return to Jamaica to retire and live in his old neighborhood."

Piper nodded. "Got it. So, is it a renovation or a new build?"

"New build," Larry said, "Edgar has made several attempts to renovate the old place, but his nephew Louis Green, has always found a way to direct the funds to something else. So, he turned to my mother for help. He will send us the funds, and we are to oversee the project. We'll have to build before or beside the current house."

Piper laughed. "This Louis person sounds like a crook."

"He is well known for his trickery, but he is his uncle's closest relative in Jamaica, and he does live at the house, which means we will probably see him.

"The house in question was one of the older types in Cascade Hills. It was built in the 20s and has housed members of the Green family since then. It was built on a stone foundation and made entirely of cedar wood. It had a pretty latticework pattern on the wraparound veranda. Luckily it was on enough land that they could build before it without interfering with the old house. Though he loved modern designs, he had a soft spot for the older buildings that had withstood hurricanes and stormy weather and were still standing and still looked pretty.

Louis was sitting on the veranda reading what looked like a Bible. Piper had to take a phone call so, Larry left her to it.

He exited the car alone, and Louis grinned when he saw him.

"Larry, I haven't seen you in ages."

Larry nodded. "That's not necessarily a bad thing. The last time I saw you, I gave you ten thousand dollars toward an imaginary eye surgery."

Louis laughed. "What can I say, Larry? I was healed. It was a miracle, man. I was so grateful I gave all the money to a church."

Larry snorted.

"You don't believe me?" Louis asked. "You don't believe I have turned over a new leaf."

"Of course not," Larry said, "and obviously, your uncle doesn't believe that you have changed either. He sent us to build on the land; working on this house with you was a lost cause. He says you are not to be involved in anything regarding the new build."

Louis nodded. "I am so sorry he thinks that way, but I have turned over a new leaf. I am even studying to be a minister. Don't you see me reading my Bible?"

"They say actions speak louder than words," Larry said. "Reading your Bible, and quoting scripture means nothing."

"I am about action, man," Louis said proudly, "I started doing ministerial things. I married a pastor and his bride."

"You did?" Larry raised an eyebrow. "Do you even have a license to marry people?"

"I applied for my license a year ago but haven't gotten it yet; the Registrar General Department is dragging their feet on this one. They have started investigating the people they give licenses to. That's a waste of government money if you ask me."

Larry sighed.

"I could be making money hand over fist by now," Louis muttered, "I made a cool ten thousand dollars just by marrying the pastor. If I had known it was so lucrative, I would have been marrying people left, right, and center long ago."

"Whoever you married is not legally married if you have no license," Larry said dismissively. "You should get your license before thinking of doing that for any other couple. You should tell the couple you supposedly married about that little technicality, by the way."

"The man I just blessed knows my license is not ready." Louis chuckled. "He didn't seem to care that I had no license. Some people are so eager for marriage that they don't care about those things. It's been bothering me, though. I don't think I gave such a good performance. I was coughing like crazy that day. I had a hay fever flare-up. And their vows were so weird, never heard a marriage vow like that. It's like they were pledging to be friends or something. I am getting too old for this world, and I am only twenty-seven."

"Is that so?" Larry asked. "Who were they?"

"That girl up Crimson Hill that looks like a fat Halle Berry and that Pastor Charming. I can't get over his last name, man. I was so surprised when he came to me and asked me to do it. I thought you would ask one of his ministerial bodies. I thought he had like two doctorates, or was it three?

"How did he have the time or energy to do one of those things, much less three? Or was it four?"

"Sorry about that; what did I miss? Piper opened the car door.

Larry was too stunned to react. Jill and Charming were not really married. That's all he heard since Louis started rambling. Charming knew about it but not Jill.

Larry started laughing. A sense of relief so pure was washing over him.

Piper was looking at him curiously, and Louis was licking his lips in Piper's direction.

"I was, uh, just telling Larry here that I am a minister of religion. I don't know why he finds it so funny."

Piper rolled her eyes, "You must be Louis Green."

"I am," Louis nodded, "what did he tell you about me?"

"Just that your uncle doesn't trust you to oversee the new building in his absence," Larry said, sobering up. "Let's get to it. Show us around; we need to take some pictures."

Chapter Fifteen

"So, to recap," Lee said, "Jill, you have all the tools to lose the weight at your disposal. I worked out an 80/20 nutrient dense menu for you, where you will eat whole unprocessed or minimally processed foods eighty percent of the time and the other twenty percent is flexible."

"Yes, I love it, it's doable." Jill said, "I can do that easily. I was shocked that you didn't put me on a weird diet where I would be restricted from certain foods."

"I don't encourage my clients to diet." Lee said. "Those who are most successful at keeping the weight off just make some adjustments to their regular way of eating, whether it's the time they eat or portion size, and keep the processed foods to a minimum. This means your cakes and pastries are occasional treats, not an everyday thing you reach for when stressed."

Jill nodded. "I understand."

"And I know that this is an unpopular opinion in this

house," Lee said, glancing at Dacy, who was chewing the protein bars Jill had baked with much enthusiasm, "but I don't think you need protein bars."

"I don't want you to depend on sugars as a snack, whether real or fake. For extra protein, drink the no sugar added protein powder, and if you want extra sweetness add berries or bananas. There will be no pastries for the first three months of your weight loss regimen."

"How on earth will I manage?" Jill fretted.

"It gets easier after a week or two," Larry said, "but sugar withdrawal is a milder version of when I quit smoking. But, to keep you honest, I'll probably need to be your shadow in those first couple of days."

"He speaks," Jill said, "you have been so pensive and quiet."

Larry smiled absently, "I have a lot on my mind, and I was respecting the professional counsel given to you by Lee. He has practical expertise in this; I don't."

"Thank you, Larry," Lee grinned. "I sent you Jill's exercise schedule by phone."

Larry took out his phone. "Two-mile walk daily, and three days of weight training with light weights. You are being easy on her."

"I want this to be a habit," Lee said, "walking a mile to a destination and then walking back is an easy commitment, and we'll ramp up the weights as she gets stronger. This is a marathon, not a sprint. I don't want you to change anything until I assess her feelings."

"Okay," Larry drawled. "Is this it? I am going to bounce. I have a ton of things to do."

"On a Saturday night!" Dacy protested. "Don't go. Have a protein bar."

"No thanks." Larry got up and stretched.

Jill looked at him helplessly. Why did he have to be so fine? And why was she still so very aware of him.

"We are going to play truth or dare," Dacy said, "I invited Rodney Charming to come to games night."

"You did what?" Jill protested. "Dacy!"

"I think we should get to know your husband," Dacy said, "Lee and I are leaving in a few days. I have no idea who he is on a personal basis. I think we should make an effort to get to know him. Besides, there is a sentiment among those closest to you that he is not to be trusted. I want to be settled in my mind before I leave you at his mercy."

Dacy looked at Larry significantly. "I think we should try to get to know the man before we judge him."

"Suddenly, I am intrigued," Larry sat back down. "I've never played truth or dare before."

"Are you serious?" Dacy asked, "never?"

"Never," Larry nodded. "My idea of a party game is dominoes."

"Mine too," Lee said, "truth or dare is basically asking a bunch of questions. If you don't want to answer truthfully, you must do a dare instead. And this is the couple's edition, where you are asked all kinds of awkward personal questions that I frankly do not like."

"Here are the cards," Dacy carried the stack of cards to the living room. They were in bi-colors, green and red.

She read from the top card on the pile. "Do you feel you should have married someone else?"

"And then, if the person doesn't answer truthfully. The dare would be to perform a seductive dance on a nursery rhyme."

"I don't want to play," Jill said.

"I like it," Larry rubbed his hands together. "So aren't you going to answer Jill?"

Jill sighed. "Well, I don't want to make a fool of myself dancing seductively to a nursery rhyme."

"So answer the question," Larry prompted.

"Yes," Jill growled, "satisfied?"

Larry nodded. "Oddly, yes."

Dacy laughed. "You haven't been married a week. Give it time."

"I need a partner," Larry whipped out his phone, "I can't be here alone answering questions without a partner."

So who are you going to call? Jill asked sharply.

"My partner in crime." Larry chuckled, "Mercedes."

"She is your sister; that's no fun," Dacy snorted, "spice it up and call that new girl you are working with."

"Piper?" Larry raised an eyebrow. "How did you know about her?"

"Jill told me," Dacy said cheekily. "She is jealous of the two of you."

"No, I am not," Jill said.

"Truth or dare," Dacy giggled. "Have you ever been jealous of Piper Miller and Larry Nelson together? Do you stay up nights and fret that you are losing him to Piper?"

"What's the dare?" Jill asked, trying to avoid Larry's grinning face.

"Call Piper and invite her to games night," Dacy said.

Jill inhaled. "What's her number, Larry?"

Larry laughed, "I think I am going to like this game. You would rather invite Piper to games night than admit you have the hots for me, and you are jealous of her."

"That's right," Jill growled.

He gave Jill the number and watched as she actually made the call. Piper must have agreed because Jill was giving her directions.

"She was just leaving Silver Spoon Restaurant to head

home and was happy for the invite." Jill said, "I am happy I invited her; she sounded so grateful to be included."

"Well then, let the games begin." Larry looked at Jill, "I am hoping your new husband is truthful and does none of the dares."

****

Rodney had no idea why he had accepted Dacy's invitation to a game night. He had a sermon to prepare for, and he had to search for his notes on Hermeneutics. He had promised Pastor Hunt to do the classes in his stead this year at the Bible College in Montego Bay.

He shouldn't be relaxing and playing games. But he was curious about Jill's friends, especially, Dacy. He was curious about her time in prison and her back story as Canon Bishop's illegitimate child. He was also curious about her husband, Lee Wiley. Was he related to C. Wiley, the gospel singer?

Besides, he wanted to see what the living residence of Golden Acres looked like. He had never been to that part of the new retirement hotel before.

He drove to the residential entrance, was waved through by a security guard, and was in open-mouthed astonishment at the time it took for him to find townhouse three. They built a nice community for their workers. The houses were modern and looked like where he used to live. A sense of nostalgia gripped him.

He wouldn't think about that now. He put his game face on and knocked on door three.

Lee answered. "Pastor Charming."

"Call me Rodney," he said, smiling.

Lee nodded. "Welcome, we were waiting for you."

Rodney stepped into the foyer and then around to where the open-plan living room was. There were more people there than he had expected. His eyes skimmed over the group; they were sitting on the floor on cushions around a center table- Jill, Dacy, Larry, and Piper. Lailah's cousin Piper?

He blinked. "Hello, everyone," He said politely, hoping that he was hiding his surprise well.

"Call him Rodney," Lee said to the group.

"Hey, Rodney." He was greeted enthusiastically by everyone except Larry, he noted.

"Welcome to our home," Dacy said. "And games night."

"I haven't been to a game's night in ages." He smiled at Jill.

She smiled back. That was a relief. He hadn't seen her in person since they exchanged vows. He didn't know if she was still cooperative.

Piper was shaking her head. "You look just like Roderick. I feel as if I am looking at Roderick."

Rodney smiled. "Hello, Piper."

"You remember me?" Piper asked.

"Of course," Rodney nodded, "Lailah and Roderick's wedding, you were the maid of honor, and I was the best man."

"I am so sorry for your loss," Piper said, "Roderick was a great guy; he made my cousin happy."

"How is she?" Rodney asked.

"Out of her mind with grief. Last night she told me she didn't know if she could go on."

Rodney swallowed. "Really?"

"Yep." Piper nodded. "I am trying to convince her to come out here for a change of scenery. Have you spoken to her since your brother's death?"

"No," Roderick said, "I was in the hospital for a while after the accident. I had temporary amnesia. By the time my memory returned, quite some time had passed."

"I had no idea you were hurt so bad." Jill gasped.

"I was." Rodney turned to her. "I was in a coma for a few days. I almost suffered the same fate as my brother."

"Oh no," Jill whispered sympathetically.

"Oh, give me a break," Larry snorted. "He is alive and here now. Are we playing or what?"

****

The game progressed for a while. It was too tame, in Larry's opinion. The questions were mild, and the dares were not daring enough.

He almost rubbed his hands with glee when it was his time to question Rodney. He would ask his own questions.

"Be gentle with me," Rodney laughed when Larry picked up his card from the pile. Everybody laughed.

Larry nodded. "Ah, this one is easy. What is the most illegal thing you have ever done?"

"Illegal?" Rodney chuckled.

"As in contrary to the law, criminal, illicit," Larry said helpfully.

Everybody was lounging quietly, waiting for him to answer.

Rodney cleared his throat, clearly looking uncomfortable. "What's the dare?"

"Really, Rodney?" Dacy said lightheartedly. "Come on, that should be easy for you to answer, you are a pastor, a man of God."

"The dare is to passionately kiss the person sitting to your left," Larry said.

Rodney visibly recoiled. Jill was sitting to his left.

Jill looked horrified as well.

"Are you sure you two are married?" Piper asked after tense seconds.

"We are, but we have an understanding, isn't that right, Jill?" Rodney turned to smile at Jill.

Jill cleared her throat. "We do have an understanding."

Larry chuckled. "They are the weirdest couple ever."

"I'd say," Piper grinned.

"What do I do if I don't want to do the truth or the dare?" Rodney asked.

"I throw in my card and ask you another question," Larry said.

"Okay, let's do that." Rodney sat up straighter.

"Is there anything you do not intend to share with your partner?"

Rodney was once again fidgeting. "I really dislike this game."

"The dare is to pour cold water on your head," Larry said.

Rodney shrugged. "I don't want to do that either."

Larry threw in his card, "well then, the next question is, do you have a secret tattoo?"

"I do," Rodney said.

"Tell us more." Piper and Dacy said almost at the same time.

Rodney laughed, relieved that he was no longer in the hot seat. "You can't tell anyone at church this, but I did get a tiny tattoo of a flower on my ankle a long time ago."

"Let me see it," Dacy said.

Rodney hiked up his pants and pulled down his socks.

"What is that, a rose?" Larry asked.

"Actually, it's a lilac," Rodney said. "Whose turn is it next?"

Chapter Sixteen

Piper was waiting for Larry in his office after the Monday morning work progress meeting with his father.

"Sorry it took so long," Larry said, walking in, "but there is another big project on the horizon; you and I will have to finalize five projects this week. I am giving you the Gerard Green project. Do you think you can manage that?"

"Sure. Of course." Piper nodded.

"Do a mockup and let me see what you have." Larry sat at his desk and opened his laptop. "We are going to have a hectic couple of months."

"I've been thinking of moving to Crimson Hills," Piper said. "The rent is cheaper than here in Falmouth. I can get one of those pretty little stone houses, three bedrooms with my own yard space for half the price of my townhouse is in Falmouth."

"It is a lovely place," Larry said, "nice neighborhood. I love it there."

"I know." Piper smiled. "I really sold it to Lailah last night. I went on and on about how cool it was, how beautiful the views were, and how quiet the neighborhood was. She is coming out in six weeks. She has some loose ends to tie up. Apparently, she went back to teaching part-time at the community college. And here I was thinking she had nothing doing over there."

"Good for her," Larry said. "Crimson Hills will make her heal."

"I also wanted her to see Rodney." Piper sighed. "I know he's married to Jill, but…."

"He is not married to Jill," Larry gritted out. "Their relationship is a sham."

"Oh," Piper mused, "I did wonder about that, how weird they were acting. He didn't even want to kiss his wife, and Jill couldn't keep her eyes off you. She stares at you longingly like she can't help herself, and she hardly looks at him at all. When she does, she is not confident or assertive or acts like someone who even knows him."

"She stares at me longingly?" Larry smiled. "Really!"

"Yep," Piper nodded. "You look at her too like she is your last meal, and you are a hungry man."

Larry laughed.

"The tension between you two could be cut with a knife. And everybody within your vicinity can pick up on it. I have not had that sort of intense attraction with anyone since… ever. I only see it in movies and when you and Jill are in the same room."

"It's not that bad," Larry said.

"Oh yes, it is," Piper said, "it is that bad. I envy Jill. She has a successful business, great friends, and two men in her radius who will make any hot-blooded woman step back and blush. One of them is a successful hotty that I work with, and she does all of this while not watching her carbs or sugar intake. Who said big girls did not have things going on."

"You should tell this to Jill. She doesn't see herself as enviable," Larry laughed. "By the way, thank you. I don't mind being called a successful hotty."

Piper grinned. "I thought you were the hottest guy I had ever seen when I saw you first, then I went to Crimson Hill, and I see that you are just one of many. I met Garwin and Gersham Silver Saturday night. And after seeing Lee Wiley, ooh child, I know I have to move to Crimson Hills. It is a single girl's paradise, even to just look at you guys. That's why I told Lailah to get out here fast. I want to see how much grieving she can do with all of you around."

Larry hooted with laughter.

"How much of a sham marriage is Rodney and Jill in?" Piper asked. "Are we talking annulment on the horizon, a two-year divorce, or a separation situation?"

"None of the above," Larry said, "they are not legally married; he got a fake minister to perform the ceremony and signed fake documents. Jill knows nothing of this, though. I am trying to find the right time to tell her."

"That's why he didn't want to answer that illegal question you asked." Piper mused.

"Yup, I made that question up," Larry chuckled. "I wanted to see how he would react, and he didn't bat an eyelash, just refused to answer."

"His reaction was telling," Piper said. "I wonder what else he is hiding. He didn't answer that second question about what you intend not to share with your partner."

"I don't know," Larry said, "as long as he doesn't hurt Jill in the short term, we are good."

"But what would a supposed law-abiding clergyman be

hiding?” Piper drummed her fingers on the desk. “Maybe I should tell Lailah not to come. I did tell her that I met Rodney and that, more than anything, really pushed her to want to come. I don't want her hurt twice by the same face.”

“Leave it,” Larry said, “let her come.”

“The truth is, I can't do anything about it now,” Piper said, “once I said Rodney was out here, wild horses couldn't hold her back; we are in for some interesting times ahead.”

****

“Larry Nelson, reporting for duty,” Larry announced when he stepped into the bakery. The closed sign was up, but he knew Jill was around. She was sitting at one of the tables scrolling through her phone.

“I was looking for music,” she looked up at him and smiled.

“No need for that,” Larry leaned on the wall, “we can talk; it makes it go easier. I worked out the route: one mile to the school, two miles to the church, three miles to Crimson Hill Rest, four miles to my house, and five miles to Crimson Hill Great House. If you decide to walk to any of those locations and back, you can rack up quite a few miles.”

“I walked it to Crimson Hill Rest one night. I couldn’t speak when I arrived,” Jill said, “I had to be driven back, so embarrassing. My knees could not unlock for weeks afterward.”

Larry chuckled. “We don’t want that; we are just heading to the school tonight. I don’t want you out of commission before you begin.”

Jill locked up the store, and they started uphill. Larry kept a strolling pace. “So, how was the dinner party for you and your husband?”

"Awful," Jill said, she was getting breathless already, and they weren't even walking that fast. "Jane arranged it to be potluck style, and she did most of the cooking. And let's just say cooking is not her thing. They gave speeches about me and Rodney that were so over the top and fake, and one girl, Pastor Hunt's daughter, came up to me and told me that I did not deserve to have him; he was hers. She made a spectacle of herself; the elders had to take her outside and talk to her."

Larry chuckled. "I should have come just to see that."

"You wouldn't last a minute," Jill said, "Rodney preached about honesty, and for the life of me, I couldn't get into the sermon. I remember he skipped over the questions about illegality and keeping things from his partner."

"Red flags," Larry murmured.

"Yes," Jill sighed, "bright red."

"Regretting your decision yet?" Larry asked.

"Oh yes," Jill said, "I thought about it, and I don't think I like him all that much. Why did I think he was perfect for me? Because of that stupid game I think he is a shady individual."

"That is why we encourage our young people to get to know the person they are planning to spend the rest of their lives with," Larry said, putting on a posh accent. "People are complex creatures, and some of their foibles can be tolerated and some you can't live with. It's best to know from the courting stage. I could have been married a hundred times before I met my wife, but I was not going to let the rabid passions of lust overwhelm my higher thoughts."

Jill laughed. "You sound just like Pastor Astor. He was my guidance counselor in high school. I think he used us as his sounding board. I know too much about him and his wife, Herma."

"The pastor couldn't get away with rambling in our

sessions," Larry chuckled. "I was always prepared for him. When he wised up with me, he also came prepared. Our classes were lit. I still visit him now that he is retired."

"You still visit him?" Jill asked. "I thought you disliked pastors."

"Not as a group, just individuals who are not living up to their spiritual leadership role." Larry said. "Pastor Astor is one of the rare, good men in the ministry; he still cracks me up with his stories. He is highly entertaining. Herma says he is always happy days after a visit from me. I have him researching subjects and chasing her down the hallway, acting all young and sprightly."

Jill laughed. "I can just imagine him chasing her too; they have a genuine, enviable relationship."

"He reminds me of my father's father, John Nelson," Larry said. "They had the same spirit. Always up to an intellectual challenge and very fun-loving. Your church should have asked Pastor Astor to fill in for Pastor Hunt instead of your husband."

"You just had to remind me that I am married, didn't you?" Jill sighed.

"The question is, why are you trying to forget so soon after you made the monumental decision to tie yourself to him?"

"Where are your father's parents?" Jill changed the subject. "You rarely mention them."

"So marriage is a pain point, I see," Larry murmured. "To answer your blatant change in topic, my grandparents died a long time ago. Grandma went first, and then gramps went into a deep depression. He just slept away on the veranda while reading the newspaper, no illness just missed his girl. He died of a broken heart."

"Aw," Jill murmured, "how long were they married?"

"Ten years," Larry chuckled, "I was in the wedding photo."

"Oh really?" Jill laughed.

"Yup, their children decided to legitimize things," Larry said, "but they were together for sixty-two years in total. Quite a feat."

"Yep," Jill said.

"I guess you and Charming won't be together for that long, though," Larry said lightly.

"I would be surprised if we last sixty-two days," Jill grunted. "We are supposed to be getting to know each other, but he is spending his weekdays in Montego Bay for the next three months."

"Too bad," Larry said. "If he were around, you would definitely get even more red flags and dislike him even more. I wonder if his being away is a good thing or a bad thing. Or was it contrived so that he doesn't have much contact with you?"

"Maybe all of the above," Jill said grumpily. "Can we stop talking about him and me?"

"Sure," Larry said. "Let's talk about your dream wedding instead."

"My dream wedding," Jill said, "mmm, let me see. I would marry in church because I am that kind of girl, traditional. I would have at least seven bridesmaids. My colors would be navy blue and white. I would do all the little traditions. I want a sand ceremony and I want to release doves."

Larry whistled. "That's a lot of specifics."

"I've been planning it for years." Jill shrugged. "It's hard not to when I am making wedding cakes practically every day. I get ideas from others, and I imagine doing my own thing. What's your dream wedding?"

"I haven't thought about it, really," Larry said. "I don't

want to do any planning for it. I'll just show up, go through with it and look forward to the honeymoon. I want at least a month's worth of honeymoon."

Jill giggled. "You wouldn't be Larry if that wasn't your answer."

"And I wouldn't be Larry if you weren't the girl I am thinking of honeymooning with."

Chapter Seventeen

"I don't know why planning a wedding has to be so complicated," Cambria said to Jill; they were both poring over a wedding cake magazine. "I have been thinking about and planning this thing for ages."

"But we are in the final stretch," Jill said. "In three months, you will be a married woman, and we need to decide which cake we are making for your wedding?"

"I can't decide," Cambria said. "I was thinking traditional, and then I was thinking vanilla and chocolate or carrot."

"Not, carrot," Jill said. "Who does carrot at their wedding?"

"It's a thing." Cambria looked at her. "Don't you know that carrot is one of the main alternate cakes for weddings?"

Jill grinned. "I know. I have made carrot cakes for a wedding before. It wasn't for a local though. I haven't had carrot cake in a long, long time."

She licked her lips while saying it.

"And I hope you keep it that way," Cambria chuckled.

"Because you have been looking good. How is it going?"

Jill smiled. "Well, as you know, the first month was hell, but I have been consistent. I do my daily walks with Larry. We are up to four miles a day now. I am getting the hang of using the weights with the right form, and I stick to my eating plan. I make protein shakes with frozen bananas and berries. Sometimes I try to mimic whatever dessert I am craving. Like the other day, I did a chocolate, banana, and strawberry shake. It was so good. Maybe I should do one with carrot, put in some cinnamon, and a couple of raisins."

"I want to taste it," Cambria said.

"It doesn't have any sugar," Jill warned, "Lee said no sugar until I reach the three-month mark. I am getting my taste buds used to a low-sugar lifestyle."

"Makes sense." Cambria nodded. "So, how is it going with you and the pastor?"

"I haven't seen him in a while, close to a month now." Jill frowned. "He is working in Montego Bay. He is visiting other churches to speak on Sundays. I think our arrangement is dead in the water."

"Should I invite him to my wedding?" Cambria asked.

"Yes, why not?" Jill shrugged. "He'll be my official plus one."

Cambria smirked. "Everybody in Crimson Hill thinks that your marriage is a joke."

Jill sighed. "What are they saying?"

"That you are pregnant," Cambria snickered, "that's why you guys married so fast and in secret."

"I heard that one," Jill said.

"And then there is the alternative to that rumor: you are pregnant for Larry but married the pastor since you two seem to spend more time together than you and your husband. And then there is the whopper, you are pregnant, but you don't know for which one of them, and you are waiting for the baby to be born to tell."

"But I am getting smaller. How do they work that out," Jill laughed. "I don't know if I like to have such salacious rumors attached to my name."

Jill glanced at the clock. "I need to relieve Gina from the cash register so she can go for lunch; we have only one cashier today."

Cambria nodded. "No prob."

"When I return, decide on a cake and a simple, elegant design. It's my gift to you. I don't think it's right that you should make your own cake."

Cambria grinned. "I hear you."

The lunch crowd had abated quite a bit when Jill went around the cash register to take over from Gina. There were two people in line. One of them was the church secretary, Lorna, another was a pretty lady who looked very familiar.

Jill rang up Lorna's order and smiled her welcome to Crimson Hills smile to the lady.

"Hi, I am Jill Wimple, I have not seen you around here before."

"I am Lailah Miller," the lady smiled. "I am staying here temporarily."

"With your cousin Piper," Jill said. "You two resemble a bit."

"I have heard that," Lailah said, "the Miller genes are strong."

"Oh, now I know where I have seen her before," Lorna injected herself into the conversation. "Pastor Charming keeps a picture of you on his desk!"

"He does?" Both Jill and Lailah said at the same time.

Lorna nodded. "You are in a red dress, your hair is out, and the background is green."

Lailah widened her eyes. "I know that picture. I gave my husband that for his birthday. I wonder why Rodney has it?"

Jill was fascinated too. "That's odd."

"I would say," Lorna said, her eyes bright with speculation, "because he doesn't have a picture of you on his desk Jill and you guys are recently married."

Jill smirked. She just knew Lorna was gearing up to refer to her newly married state.

"Congratulations," Lailah said, "of course, Piper told me you were married to Rodney. We would have been family if Roderick," her lips trembled slightly, "hadn't died."

Jill sighed. "Thank you. Do you want to talk?"

"I don't want to intrude since you are busy," Lailah smiled wanly. "Maybe another time."

****

"I don't understand," Jill said, "why would he have a picture of Lailah on his desk."

"One more rep," Larry said brusquely, "and hold that form."

"Why are you ignoring me?" Jill asked.

"I don't like discussing your husband," Larry said cheekily.

"That's not true," Jill glared at him, "you tease me about my weird marriage all the time. You take great pleasure in pointing out that Rodney is avoiding me. News flash Larry, I am not bothered. I already made up my mind that I am getting an annulment as soon as he doesn't need the mantle of our marriage to help him. I am not interested in Rodney Charming as a love interest anymore."

"Good for you," Larry smiled, "but no serious conversations until after your workout. You don't concentrate when you are mulling over things."

Jill powered through the workout and watched Larry as he finished up his. At first, she had hated doing weights three nights per week, especially the first week when every part of her felt as if it hurt, but Larry had really held her foot to the fire.

He acted professionally in the gym, and while walking on the road, they chatted about everything and nothing.

Jill found that she could tell him anything, and he was fast becoming a confidant.

Larry was right; him helping her with her exercises and checking up on what she was eating had brought them closer than ever.

Larry would make a good husband someday to some lucky girl.

She wanted to be that lucky girl.

"I am going to shower," she said; they usually walked the five miles to his house, and then she worked out, and then he drove her back.

She used one of Larry's en suite to shower and then have a protein shake, and that was it for her for the day. It was a far cry from her schedule prior to this. She would have closed up the store, fed the cats had more than ten servings of pastries, and watch television or read a book.

Now here she was, Jill Wimple, a woman changed. And not only her eating and exercising habits. Maybe it was the shedding of the excess weight; so far, she was down fifteen pounds. The more inches and weight she dropped, the more her confidence seemed to rise out of the ashes.

She was seeing things a lot differently these days, and it was clear that she was a pushover, a pawn. She had allowed herself to be led by whoever was around her and had the most influence.

She didn't know who she was.

After a quick shower and a change of clothes, which were surprisingly loose feeling, in just a few weeks. It was quite heartening for her that pretty soon, she would have to shop for new clothes and discard her 4X clothing.

That was motivation enough for her to keep on going. Why had she thought that being married to Rodney and anticipating a honeymoon would be motivating?

She went to Larry's kitchen and made them both a smoothie. Larry's kitchen was usually well stocked when she came over, and she knew he only did it because she was going to be there. He hardly used the place since he ate breakfast and dinner at his parent's house.

Even though they had their own homes and were married like Jeremiah, all of the children went over to Bunny and Bobby's place like it was a restaurant.

If she lived on the Nelson compound, she wouldn't be doing that; she would be using Larry's state-of-the-art kitchen. It was a chef's dream. His whole place was a dream. They liked the same design aesthetic. She liked coming over to his house.

"What are you musing about?" Larry asked pulling his shirt over his head. He had obviously had a shower; he smelled like his spearmint and basil shower gel.

"I was just thinking that I like it over here," Jill answered honestly. "Your house is well designed."

"It's Jeremiah's design with a few changes."

"Yep, I remember you telling me that," Jill took a sip of her smoothie.

"Want us to hang for a while?" Larry asked.

"Sure." Jill headed to the living room; she loved the cool tones, grey, white, silver, and blue. This is how she wanted to overhaul her grandmother's living space, but she was sure that Sally Wimple would return when she was tired of flitting about and visiting her family and cry bloody murder at Jill's modern overhaul of her cozy space.

Larry turned on the stereo and sat beside her, Moonlight Sonata by Beethoven came on.

"You are an enigma," Jill said, "nobody would peg you as a classical music lover."

"I used to hate it when I was younger," Larry sipped his smoothie and closed his eyes, "but the older I get, the more grateful I am that this genre of music exists. It is calming to the mind. Sometimes I need things at a slow pace to center myself."

"Are you tired?" Jill asked.

"Exhausted," Larry said, "the volume of work we are getting is unprecedented. I am happy to be home to help out, but really Nelson Construction is a high-octane company right now."

"And added to that, you are helping me with my exercise," Jill said.

"It's no problem," Larry said, "I exercise anyway. It's good to have company. Your company."

"How is it going with Piper?" Jill asked. She couldn't quite hide the jealousy in her voice.

"Piper is great; no need to be jealous of her," Larry laughed. "She is a fan of yours."

"She is?" Jill asked, "why?"

"She always says how awesome you are for owning your own business. And how you have me wrapped around your finger like a lovesick puppy."

Jill laughed. "You are not a lovesick puppy."

"I am. I talk about you entirely too much at work," Larry said.

"But don't they find it odd that I am married, and you still do that?" Jill asked.

"You are not really married, Jill," Larry said. "You are just as single and unattached as I am."

"I mean, I know we haven't consummated the relationship or anything, but I signed documents. That's what makes a marriage legal." Jill sighed. "I can't imagine why I went through with it for the life of me."

"The documents were fake. The minister was fake," Larry said, "Charming keeps a picture of Lailah on his desk because she is his one great love."

Jill gasped. "What?"

"He told me that the first night I confronted him about proposing to you. He had a competition for her with his brother when they were all in grad school. Lailah chose his brother, and he was devastated. There was no hope of him eventually growing to love you. He already has his sights set on Lailah. I believe he is waiting to clear his name in Canada before approaching Lailah. And as for that pastor, it was Louis Green from Cascade Hills. He bragged about how he officiated his first wedding with Charming and a fat Halle Berry."

"Oh goodness," Jill put down the glass with the smoothie and laughed. "You mean, you knew this all along and had me going around for six weeks thinking I was an adulteress for thinking about you every night?"

"You think about me every night?" Larry asked huskily.

"In the day too, and with vivid details."

Larry smiled. "I like that."

"Of course, you would," Jill scoffed, "Louis Green called me a fat Halle Berry?"

"Sorry to offend." Larry touched her knee.

Jill laughed out loud, "I am not offended. I am flattered, really. I would be even more flattered if I looked anything like Halle Berry. All I am leaving with is that he is blind as well as a crook?"

"I don't know; maybe I need to look closer." Larry leaned into her until they were nose tip to nose tip.

"I am mad at you for not telling me that I was in a fake marriage," Jill murmured.

"It helped you to resist me," Larry said, "you can't be mad at that, you stick to your principles, and I respect that you were determined to stick to your fake commitment. Admittedly, I only came to that conclusion when I found out it wasn't real. Because when I thought you had married that guy, devastated does not begin to describe how I felt.

"If you want to be mad, I am not the one you should be mad at. I didn't lie to you."

"So what now?" Jill asked. "What do I do about Rodney? If I say anything he loses his job."

"Let him lose it." Larry shrugged.

"I can't be that heartless. He is not a bad person."

"How do you figure that?" Larry pulled away from her. "What in all of this has you blinded to that man's true character."

"I sense that he is not bad," Jill said. "I have a soft spot for his plight. What if it were my father who was accused of something like that? I wouldn't mind if somebody bought him time to clear his name."

"You are entirely too soft on this guy," Larry said. "You sense that he is not bad, and I sense that he is hiding something. I have a theory about Charming. Call me fanciful, but I think he killed his brother."

"Woah," Jill frowned. "We are going from fake marriage to murder."

"It's not impossible," Larry said, "his brother left America to go to Canada, to meet with him, and next thing we know they are in a car accident. Did he cause the accident hoping to kill his brother so that he could have Lailah?"

"You watch too many detective shows," Jill said.

"I think we should set up a sting," Larry said eagerly. "And get him to confess exactly what he did. I can't lose the feeling that something is wrong with him, and I need to know what it is."

"Like a dog with a bone," Jill sighed. "How would we go about this? Play another truth or dare game?"

"That wouldn't work," Larry murmured. "He doesn't answer any of the questions he doesn't want to. I'll think of something."

Chapter Eighteen

"**W**here is the rest of you?" Dacy squealed when Jill opened her apartment door a few weeks later.

Dacy was back from St. Lucia; they were supposed to go shopping at Nessa's to get outfits for Cambria's wedding.

Jill had to shop for other outfits, too; she had lost thirty-five pounds in four months and had gained a ton of confidence.

"I can't believe it," Dacy said, tears in her eyes. "You are looking more than good."

"I feel good too." Jill hugged her friend. "For the first time in my life, I am losing weight without fasting or frenzied inconsistent exercise. And I am managing my snacking."

"I think you will lose the hundred pounds in a year," Dacy said, "and then what?"

"And then nothing." Jill laughed. "I am not really married. I told you this over the phone. There will be no grand honeymoon because it was all fake."

"And you haven't told Rodney that you know yet?" Dacy

asked.

"No," Jill said, "he is hardly around, and when he calls, I find ways to avoid him."

"It's weird," Dacy said. "Are you sure he is still around?"

"Quite sure, he even preached at church Sunday, or so I heard. I didn't go. I am quite reluctant to face people when I know that I am not really married to the pastor. I vacillate between being happy and being mad that Larry told me. I am hopeless at acting."

"Let's go," Dacy said. "You can tell me more in the car."

"And you can tell me more about St. Lucia," Jill said. "I like the pictures you sent."

Nessa personally greeted them in the store when they got there. She looked at Jill in awe, "I can see the weight loss; your face is looking streamlined already. Are those cheekbones? Go girl, good progress.

"When buying clothes, I think you should buy just a few things at every stage. You can go hog wild when you get to your ideal weight. I will personally shop for clothes that I think you would like to dress that fabulous coca cola bottle shape of yours."

"It's called an hourglass figure, Nessa," Dacy laughed. "I can't tell you how many cat calls Jill got when she walked from the car to the store."

"They were calling to you," Jill said bashfully.

"No honey buns, it was you," Dacy said. "You have always been pretty but losing the extra weight makes people sit up and take notice."

"And you had better get used to it," Nessa said, "you have naturally what people pay good money for. I have a customer who recently did a Brazilian butt lift; that is all she talks about. That pastor man of yours will have to beat off the crowd."

Jill cleared her throat, "Nessa, we are not exactly married. It's a long story."

"Thank God, never liked him for you," Nessa said jovially. "Tell you what, one day, when I am in your vicinity, we can have a cup of coffee and talk."

"Sure thing," Jill nodded, "do you have anything appropriate for me for a wedding?"

"Oh yes, you would like conservative but flirty. I have just the thing for you. This way." Nessa said cheerfully. They both followed Nessa while she rifled through the clothes on the rack that she had isolated just for Jill and Dacy.

"Hi Jill," Lailah said behind them.

"Lailah!" Jill smiled, "I thought you were in Kingston."

"I was, but I came back yesterday." Lailah grimaced, "I don't want Piper to spend the holidays alone."

"Lailah meet Dacy and Nessa," Jill introduced the women.

Lailah smiled at Dacy. "Lovely to meet you. I heard your story."

"It's crazy, huh?" Dacy said. "So, how are you enjoying your vacation so far?"

"It's good," Lailah said, "a change of scenery is just what the doctor ordered for my grieving soul. I was cooped up in the apartment in New York and afraid to move any of his things."

"Is Rodney back yet, Jill? I would love to run into him this time around. I know he is not my husband, but I would love to see his face."

"He is supposed to be back today," Jill said. "Cambria's wedding is this weekend. He is invited."

Nessa held up a beige dress with some lilac flower patterns on it. "Now this is whimsical and flirty, crisscross bodice, sink in the waist, flared at the hips. It will look good on you, Jill."

"If you had one in my size, I would get it," Lailah said, "it's littered with lilacs, my favorite flower. I even have a tattoo."

She raised her pant leg.

Both Dacy and Jill looked at the neat little flower on her ankle.

"I actually got it done to match Roderick's tattoo," Lailah said, "I made him get a mole tattoo on his neck so that I could tell him apart from Rodney. He also got a lilac to match mine."

Dacy looked at Jill.

Jill looked back at her, stunned. Rodney had that same tattoo. Why did he get a tattoo to match his brother's?

"It's cute," Jill was the first to drag herself out of the shock.

"Er…do you have that dress in my size?" Dacy hurriedly changed the subject.

****

"**W**e found the girl; she is well over the age of consent. How do you want me to proceed?"

Michael's voice rang in his head as Rodney maneuvered the car into the unexpected Falmouth traffic. It was the time of year, when traffic was crazy on the road. It was one week before Christmas. He could smell and taste the freedom before him.

He wanted to hop on a plane and go to Canada right now, sort out loose ends, and repair his reputation, but first, he needed to stop hiding from Lailah, give her a visit, and lay it all on the line. He would convince her to marry him, and they could move to another state and then start afresh elsewhere. Never to part again.

But first, he would have to tell Jill Wimple goodbye,

tell her thank you for her selfless act in marrying him but then confess that they weren't really married. He would tell Crimson Hill church goodbye. They weren't a bad bunch of folks. He would thank his uncle Noel for his brilliant plan to keep him employed, and then he would leave. He had no intention of ever returning to Jamaica. It had been an interesting adventure, and no doubt he would miss aspects of the place, but he had spent the past year acting in a role that he didn't particularly like.

It had been exhausting being Rodney Charming, pastor and religious scholar with two PhDs. His little stint at the bible college these past months was even worse than his post as temporary pastor at Crimson Hill Baptist. He had wrestled with a group of men and women who were too bright for their own good. He was glad that was over. No doubt they would not be giving him any rave reviews in their teacher assessment.

He exited Falmouth and turned on to Crimson Hills main road; his days of pretense were nearly over. But first, he had a wedding to attend with Jill as his date.

****

Cambria and Jack Knight's wedding was a fairytale-themed event at one of the gazebos on Knights Bridge Farm. Rodney had agreed to meet Jill there and did a double take when he saw Jill step out of her vehicle.

She looked different. She was looking shapelier and fit. Her most dramatic transformation was her face. The double chin was gone. He felt a reluctant surge of attraction for the gorgeous woman she was shaping up to be. For just a minute, he contemplated making it real with her. He would have made it with Jill if any of this was real. They would have worked. But it wasn't real, and he already loved someone else.

Jill was attracting quite a bit of attention, too, with her arrival. But one person stood out, Larry Nelson. He was looking at her with a kind of possessiveness and love that Rodney knew he couldn't match even if he tried. It was blazing from his eyes.

Jill sought Larry out in the crowd and waved enthusiastically, smiling wide when she saw him.

Larry blew a kiss in her direction, and she blushed like a schoolgirl. Rodney was superfluous to requirements. He was going to tell Jill before the evening was over that they weren't really married and thank her for helping him out. He didn't want to be the specter between Jill and Larry any longer. He needed to come clean and let them love each other in freedom.

He went to join her, complimenting her profusely.

"Thank you, Rodney," she said. Her smile was not as wide or enthusiastic for him as it was for Larry, he noted.

It was a spectacular wedding, simple and elegant, with some of the most sumptuous food he had tasted in a while. His uncle Noel found him at the bar. He was nursing a virgin pina colada for minutes while chit-chatting with several women. Some of them he recognized from the district, and some were obviously visitors.

"You should be with your wife," Noel said to him sternly. "She is spending way too much time with Larry Nelson while you are over here. Is there trouble in paradise already?"

Rodney smiled at his uncle. "There was never any paradise, to begin with, and you know that. Today was the first time I have seen Jill in the past three months. I had that pesky teaching gig to do, and she has been avoiding me like the plague."

"She is looking different, isn't she?" Noel said. "I can't get over it. Maybe I should lose some weight," he patted his belly.

Rodney chuckled. "Uncle Noel, I want to tell you thank you for looking out for me. You really stood in my corner this past year, but I am happy to announce that they found the girl. Her real name is Rose, and she is twenty-six. She was paid to get dirt on me to remove me from the university presidential race. My lawyer is taking steps to clear my name. I may be suing her because I want it on the record that she tried to ruin my reputation."

"Say what?" Noel said gruffly. "That's good news. I always knew you weren't a pedophile."

"I know you believed in me," Rodney sighed. "I am thinking of leaving soon, though."

"As I expected when this happened, I will clear it with the elders," Noel said. "So, are you taking Jill with you?"

"No," Rodney said, "the marriage was not legal, and it is not what Jill would want. Look at her."

Noel looked over to where he was pointing. Jill and Larry were dancing close, oblivious to anybody else around them.

"I see that," Noel muttered. "I am most disappointed in Sister Jill. I thought she would have chosen someone who was more suitable."

"You mean like me?" Rodney laughed. "A man of the cloth, with a womanizing reputation a mile long, that can't settle down to save his life. If I were to advise a woman on who to choose between Larry and me, I would tell her to choose Larry."

Noel cleared his throat. "Well, when you put it that way."

"Larry is quite fine for her, perfect even," Rodney sighed, "just like Lailah was perfect for me. If I had stayed with Lailah, I wouldn't have the reputation I have, that's if she had chosen me. I figure it will be the same for Larry. He has found his person."

"I saw Lailah; she visited me and Jane yesterday. She said you were avoiding her."

"I was," Rodney nodded. "I didn't want to meet her with a cloud hanging over me; now it's gone."

"I see," Noel slapped his shoulder. "I wish you all the best, Rodney."

****

Rodney followed Jill home, driving closely behind her. She parked in the parking lot and got out of her vehicle.

"Whew, that was quite a party!" She grinned at him. "I didn't see you for most of the night."

"I know you were having a good time with Larry and your girlfriends. I didn't want to intrude."

Jill smiled. "So what do you want to talk to me about?"

"We are not really married," Rodney decided to come out with the truth and not beat around the bush.

"I know," Jill said. "Larry told me. He met Louis Green some weeks ago, and he blabbed about it."

"I am sorry," Rodney said. "I should have let you know."

"It's okay," Jill said, "you wanted the time to clear your name. I didn't mind giving it to you. Besides, if I had known, I couldn't have acted as if I didn't know."

"My name is finally being cleared," Rodney said. "I will be leaving here soon to make sure everything goes according to plan. Thank you for everything, Jill."

"Oh, I am happy for you," Jill said. "I have been meaning to ask you this, though. It has been on my mind. Why do you have the same matching lilac tattoo as Lailah?"

"Oh, the tattoo," Rodney shrugged, "we did it back in

college."

"She got a matching tattoo with both you and her husband?" Jill asked skeptically.

"Yes, it would seem so," Rodney said. "Lailah and I dated each other before. That's when I got it."

Jill nodded. "Okay. I am glad that is cleared up. When she showed us her tattoo, Dacy and I wondered about it."

"She's back here in Crimson Hills?" Rodney asked.

"Yes." Jill said. "She wants to see you."

Rodney smiled. "Well then, I'll see her. Have a good night, Jill."

Jill nodded. "You have a good night too."

Chapter Nineteen

"**I** am telling you, Larry," Jill panted as they kept up a brisk pace over the hill. "Lailah showed us a lilac tattoo identical to the one on Rodney's foot. I asked him about it last night, and he said he got the exact same tattoo as his brother and Lailah. How do you explain that?"

"He killed his brother and copied his tattoo, trying to make himself over into being his brother," Larry said. "At least it's something that he finally had the decency to tell you the truth about your sham marriage, though."

"I guess," Jill said, "something about the whole tattoo story is not sitting well with me. We should just go and ask him. We are close to the manse."

"And let him know we suspect him of murder. Oh no," Larry shook his head, "he is a dangerous man. Maybe he will kill us too."

"You suspect him of murder, I don't." Jill pointed out. "I just think he is obsessed with his brother's wife. And probably copied everything he did. Maybe he did the tattoo to confuse her. He does have that tattooed mole at the side of his neck too. Once Lailah said it, it is easy to spot."

"You want the softer explanation because you still like the guy," Larry muttered.

"I don't still like him. I am not sure I ever really did." Jill growled. "You don't like him, so you want to accuse him of murder."

"We should call Lee as backup," Larry said, "he is a karate expert."

Jill laughed. "Back up for what? Rodney is our friendly neighborhood pastor who has a simple case of unresolved issues with his brother's wife."

"Speaking of brother's wife," Larry whispered as a car slowed down at the manse gate and paused, "isn't that Piper's car?"

"Yes," Jill whispered, "Lailah is driving, she is on the phone."

"She is probably calling him to open the gate," Larry said. "We could go in after her and see what they are up to."

Jill chuckled. "Since we started hanging again, I have done a ton of questionable things. I don't want to add trespassing to it."

"It's not trespassing if you pay your tithes," Larry said, "the church house belongs to the church; the church is the people. You, Jill, are the people."

Jill grinned. "I can't argue with that logic."

"It's opening," Larry said. "We will have to get in before the gate close and stay close to the trees in the driveway. It's a good thing we are both in dark colors tonight."

When the gates opened, they slipped in before it closed. Jill had an insane urge to laugh. The last time she acted impulsively, she had danced in the rain with Larry. She only had bouts of exhilarating, life-affirming joy around him.

"Now stick close to me," Larry whispered near her ear.

They silently crossed the lawn and went up the driveway. Lailah exited the car, looked at Rodney, and burst into tears.

"I am so sorry," she sobbed, "you look so much like him. I can't get over Roderick, and I have been trying."

Rodney hugged her to him, a tight familiar hug.

Larry squeezed her hand and murmured. "Now that's familiar."

Lailah hugged him back and they stood there for what seemed like hours.

"Let's go inside," Rodney said huskily.

"I don't think it's a good idea," Lailah pulled away. "You are married."

"I am," Rodney said, "but not to Jill. I am married to you, Lailah. It's me, Roderick!"

"What the hell?" Larry muttered.

"Rod?" Lailah seemed just as shocked as they were.

"Let's go inside," he said urgently. "I don't like talking out here. We need some privacy."

They went inside the living room and closed the door.

Jill's head was reeling.

"Okay," Larry murmured, "now this makes sense. I always knew there was something phony about him, but now I know. And now I understand. He was trying to act like his brother. It wasn't coming off well at all."

"I want to hear his story," Jill whispered. "How did he pull this off? Why did he pull this off? Oh, my word."

"Maybe if we are quiet and stand there," Larry pointed at an open window, "we'll hear the story from the horse's mouth."

They tiptoed to the living room window. Rodney was pouring Lailah a drink. Lailah looked as shocked as Jill was feeling.

"So I left for Canada and met with Rodney's lawyer Michael. Remember Rodney had claimed that Michael was the best?"

Lailah nodded. She was probably speechless poor thing.

"After the meeting, we were on our way to Rodney's house when the car picked up a skid, flipped over, and Rodney died. I was just knocked on the head and had a couple of bruises. When I woke up, I couldn't remember a thing. I didn't know who I was, whether I was Rodney or Roderick.

"For days I was in a coma, and then when I got out of it, my memories were scrambled. Michael suggested in a not-subtle way that it would be easier for me if I were Rodney. He could easily keep Rodney out of jail than he could Roderick.

"I wanted to call you; trust me, I did, but I knew I couldn't. It was better if you thought I was dead and then I approached you as my brother in the future when everything was free and clear. I am happy I chose to take up Rodney's identity. Michael was right; my coworker, Felix Alterman, got fifteen years."

Lailah nodded. "I know. A part of my grief about losing you was that you wouldn't be around anyway. Oh, Roderick, do you think you can get away with this?"

"I have so far," Roderick said, "apart from mad Maud Beecher, who seems to know things nobody else does, and Larry Nelson, whose main interest in me was because I asked Jill to marry me, there is no one else who would even think of this."

"Why did you have to marry Jill?" Lailah asked jealously. "Couldn't you find a less attractive girl?"

Jill smiled.

Larry shook his head at her and whispered. "You are so

vain."

"I married Jill because she is helpful and kind. She volunteers for everything at church. She is a devoted Christian woman; she would see my reasoning for getting married and would be willing not to act upon her marriage vows before we got to know each other. I got an out when she suggested that she needed to lose a hundred pounds. I thought that could buy me some time."

"I can't wrap my head around this," Lailah got up and hugged him. "So what are we going to do now?"

"I go back to Canada and clear up Rodney's name. No one will be surprised if I start afresh somewhere else. You go back to the States, I join you there, and then we get married. We cease this second chance. I have no idea what I will do professionally, though. It would look odd for Rodney Charming, Ph.D., to be doing accounting, and trust me when I tell you, I am not cut out to be a pastor. I tried acting like one for a year, and it was no fun."

"I know that's right," Larry murmured, "he was phony from a mile away."

"You will have to break it off with Jill," Lailah murmured.

"Already done. She didn't shed any tears trust me; she is so in love with Larry and he with her that it's a wonder that she said yes to me in the first place. I am so sorry that you had to go through this, Lailah. My heart ached when I heard how heartbroken you are. And when you were out here in the same country. I had to avoid you like the plague. I didn't want my cover to be blown."

They started kissing hungrily.

Jill turned to Larry. "Let's go. I don't want to see them doing it."

Larry chuckled. "Why ex Mrs. Charming, feeling jealous?"

"Nope," Jill said, "voyeurism is not my thing, and they are actually married to each other; one of them thought the other was dead. Let them have their privacy."

They walked to the side gate, and Larry opened it as quietly as he could.

"Are you going to expose him?" Jill asked when they were on the road.

"I don't see why I should or how I could prove any of what I just heard or even who would believe me. He was identical to his brother, so I am figuring they have the same DNA. His brother didn't leave anyone behind that would be devastated by him being dead." Larry shrugged. "Besides, Charming didn't touch you; he was harmless. I actually feel no ill will toward the guy. Come to think of it, I like him."

Jill grinned. "Okay. That's a rapid change of tune."

"Are you going to expose him?" Larry asked.

"No," Jill frowned. "I figure if he is going to be exposed one day, it's not my place to do it."

"I wonder what excuse he is going to give the church for lying to them," Larry asked.

"Who knows?" Jill said breezily.

"So what does this mean now that you are clearly single and not pretending?" Larry asked. "Are you going to let us exercise in secret now?"

"I am not ashamed of you," Jill said. "Or of us."

"So there is an us?" Larry stopped and turned to her.

Jill nodded. "Yes. You are now officially my boyfriend. I will put up a sign in the shop if you want. I'll even call my grandmother and tell her as soon as I get home."

"Is that so?" Larry smiled. "Are you sure you don't want to wait until you lose the rest of the weight to see what kind of guy you can bag? Maybe you can get another pastor with a Ph.D."

"Not interested in pastors or men with PhDs anymore," Jill said.

"That's too bad." Larry chuckled, "Because I'll have mine in two months."

"What?" Jill widened her eyes.

"It was only a couple credits to do it after my masters, so I said, what the heck." Larry shrugged. "Nobody knows about it, really. Just my parents and the guys in academia, including one Dr. Phillip Wimple."

"Are you serious?" Jill whispered. "You are working with my dad?"

"Yup." Larry nodded. "And your mother. They are cool people."

"I can't believe this." Jill laughed. "Only you would think it's a big secret to be doing a Ph.D."

"I don't like to announce these kinds of things; it messes with my street cred," Larry said, "I would be so embarrassed if someone calls me Dr. Nelson."

Jill hooked her arm in his. "From the town bad boy to Dr. Nelson. I love it. Don't worry. I won't tell anyone if you don't want me to."

"My secret keeper," Larry said happily. "I have to ask you something."

"What?" Jill turned to him

"I once did this quite sloppily and offhand, but at the time, I was a little jolted and jealous that you could even think of marrying another man when I am around," Larry said, "but that's all water under the bridge now. I have more clarity and a little bit more maturity, and I am quite sure of this; I love you, Jill. I got hooked at eighteen and never really got over it."

"And I love you, Larry," Jill said, "I am sorry that it took me this long to acknowledge it out loud."

Larry held her hands tightly. "You are the love of my life." He drew even closer to her.

"I love you unreservedly."

Jill instinctively curved closer to him and caressed her lips.

Her heartbeat went crazy in the thrumming silence.

"Larry..." she mumbled.

"I am going to do this right; we are going to court each other or date or whatever," he murmured, "and then I am going to ask you to marry me."

"Yes," Jill smiled in the night air. "I'll say yes, yes, and yes."

He captured her lips in a devouring kiss, and they stood in the middle of the road kissing each other, only coming up for air when a car passed them.

Jill groaned in Larry's chest. "I am gaining a notorious reputation in these hills."

Larry chuckled. "Are you afraid you will no longer be known as a nice girl?"

"At this point, I do not care," Jill said. "I love you so much."

****

Larry dressed in his best black suit and joined his family for breakfast.

"Where are you going?" Mercedes asked, shocked.

His parents, Jeremiah and a heavily pregnant Shay, were curious too. They all waited with various levels of anticipation to hear him answer.

"Church," Larry said. "I expect Pastor Charming will announce that he is leaving. I am interested in hearing how he will spin his story about why he is not really married to

Jill. I want all the church people to see me sitting beside her while he is telling it."

"But I wasn't planning to go today," Bunny said. "What is happening? Update us."

"I suggest that you come," Larry said.

"I can't be bothered to go and put on a suit now, Larry," Bobby complained. "So Jill is not really married to the pastor?"

"Nope," Larry said. "I found out the day after it happened."

"And you didn't say a word," Jeremiah said, "and we were all here feeling sorry for you and Jill… star-crossed lovers who got a bad deal in the romance department."

"I told you he will be fine," Shay said, rubbing her belly. "He didn't seem like a heartbroken man to me. As a matter of fact, Larry looked like he was floating on cloud nine, hanging with Jill every day."

"How do you know the pastor is leaving?" Bunny said, "he hasn't said anything to anyone."

Larry smiled. "Well…"

"Well, what?" Bunny growled. "Why is this man so secretive?"

"I like that about Larry," Shay said. "He is like a vault."

"I'll get it out of him," Mercedes said, "but I am too curious to wait ten years. I am going to put on my clothes. And if there are blanks, you had better fill it in, Lawrence Nelson. I am your sister. I deserve to know."

Larry laughed.

"I am getting ready, too," Bunny said. "Come on, Bobby."

Bobby got up obediently. "I am not wearing a suit, though."

Larry watched as his sister and his parents scrambled to leave the table to make it to church, and he laughed.

Shay put up her feet on the nearest chair and shook

her head. "Wild horses will not make me get ready to go anywhere."

Jeremiah glared at Larry. "We are your family; why can't you tell us the story?"

"It's not my story to tell." Larry shrugged. "I can tell you, though, that Charming had some trouble in Canada, and he came out here to cool out. The church said no single pastors, so he asked Jill to marry him to keep his job. He used Louis Green, a known crook, who would do anything for a buck as his marriage officiant. So they are not legally married.

"And now that Charming's problems are sorted out in Canada, he is going back to reclaim his life there, and he may be going back with his previous sister-in-law for whom he has always had a torch."

"Oh," Jeremiah frowned. "Well, that's okay then. I assume Jill is quite fine because I have seen her with you lately."

"She is just fine." Larry smiled.

****

Larry's walking into church and sitting beside Jill caused a stir with the brethren. Everyone's eyes were glued to them. Jill sat up straighter and squared her shoulders.

She hadn't heard a word from Rodney/Roderick since Sunday night, nor did she expect to. That was their goodbye.

He wasn't preaching today, Pastor Aster was. It was announced that the seasoned pastor would presumably step in until Pastor Hunt returned.

And then Pastor Charming got up. The church was understandably confused. His supposed wife was sitting in the congregation with Larry Nelson, and he was leaving.

"I know you are a bit confused," Pastor Charming said, "but I would like to start with why I am here in the first place. I was blacklisted, my reputation took a beating, and I was graciously offered a position here in the absence of Pastor Hunt. Unfortunately, you don't like your pastors single, so I asked Sister Jill Wimple to help me."

"And she did help me; we agreed that the marriage would come first, and then we get to know each other better after.

"So I got a minister to perform the ceremony quickly; in hindsight, I should have realized that all was not right with him. That person was not licensed. Sister Jill and I are not really married."

The church inhaled a collective breath.

"It is okay," Pastor Charming continued. "Sister Jill is quite happy that she has her freedom, and so is Brother Larry Nelson, I am sure."

Larry chuckled beside her. "He called me brother, how cute."

"Anyway, my situation is sorted in Canada, and I will be returning to tie up loose ends. You were a good congregation. You received me well. Thank you all for your hospitality."

The murmurs only subsided when the choir got up to sing. It was quite a bundle at the door when everybody wanted to greet the pastor and to tell him their personal goodbyes.

Jill was also bombarded by her church friends. Larry didn't leave her side. Everybody got the message. They were now a team.

"When are you two getting married?" Noel White greeted Jill with a hug and shook Larry's hand. "I have been fielding questions about your situation."

"When we are good and ready," Larry smirked.

Noel backed away when he saw the challenge in Larry's eyes.

"Jill, and Larry, welcome to church." Rodney shook their hands enthusiastically. "You two look good together."

"I just came to offer Jill some moral support," Larry said, "and to tell you to keep it aboveboard this time, huh. Make this second chance count and take good care of Lailah."

"Er…Lailah?" Rodney asked tentatively. "What do you know about Lailah and me?"

"You don't want me to answer that," Larry stared him in the face. "Your secret is safe with us, Roderick."

Rodney looked dazed.

Jill held Larry's hands, and they headed to the car.

Chapter Twenty

Six months later

Jill couldn't believe that the woman staring back at her in the mirror was her, Jill Wimple. She had lost one hundred and ten pounds in a year. The extra ten had been unexpected and was probably due to her recent addiction to running up the hill with a tire tied to her waist.

She was lean and hard and fit. A far cry from the woman she used to look like. It was still unbelievable sometimes. What was even more unbelievable was that she could fit in her grandmother's wedding dress. The simple style was timeless and only needed a few adjustments.

She had gone full traditional for her wedding. All of her family and Larry's were involved. She had four bridesmaids instead of seven because Larry begged her to cut it down.

Dacy, her matron of honor, her mother and grandmother, and Bunny were in the room with her as she got ready.

Jill had wanted all the traditional wedding things. And her

family had obliged.

"Where is my something old, new, borrowed, and blue." She asked.

"Here is your old," Sally Wimple said behind her, "I am putting it on your bouquet. It was the lace from my veil. Though your dress would qualify as old as it was mine."

"Unbelievable, how pretty it still is," Dacy said.

"I preserved it for Jill," Sally Wimple said. "I have always prayed I would see her wear it one day. And I am happy it is to marry the man you love and who loves you back without reserve."

"Grandma, do not let me cry," Jill said, blinking back tears.

Sally smiled. "I am happy for you."

"As am I," her mother said. "Though I am feeling kind of salty that Sally didn't tell me about this pretty dress when I was marrying Phillip. Here is your something new, my darling," she placed a bracelet on Jill's wrist. "I can hardly recognize you these days, and not because of the weight loss. I see an inner strength in you that was not there before. I like it."

It was a bracelet with her and Larry's name on it.

"And here is the borrowed," Bunny said, "slipping a flower in her intricately styled chignon. Now it is perfect," Bunny said mistily. "I am so happy that you are joining our family. This has always been my dream."

"And I have on my blue," Jill said, pointing to her blue shoes. Her wedding colors were navy blue and white, just like she had always planned.

"Okay, let's get this party started," Dacy said. "I am so happy that my girl is getting married, and I can be here to celebrate with you."

"Unlike that other sham marriage," Sally murmured. "I

couldn't believe when I heard what you were doing, Jill."

Jill laughed. "At least I have a story to tell my children. My romance story is not that dull after all."

She met her father in the passageway of the church, and the timeless instrumental of Here Comes the Bride came on. She marched down the aisle to her groom with the church filled with their family and friends.

"I love you, Jill," Larry whispered. "Always and forever."

"I love you, Larry, always and forever" she said, maybe a little bit too loud because everybody heard. But Jill didn't mind; it was perfect.

The End

Excerpt- No Place Like You
(Book Eight, Crimson Hill Series)

Prologue
After High School Graduation

"You can either come and work with me at Sensuous City or find a job elsewhere." Pearl pulled back the curtain aggressively and allowed the sunlight to hit Jewel squarely in the face. "We are poor people; we don't have the luxury of lounging in bed."

Jewel covered her eyes. "What time is it?"

"Seven o'clock. June thirtieth. I just got in from work," Pearl said snarkily. "Now get up and start to hustle, or I will have to kick you out. My mother kicked me out when I was your age."

"You were pregnant with me," Jewel murmured. "Where is the gratitude that I actually graduated high school?"

"Gratitude!" Pearl yelled, "if you hadn't graduated, I would have done you serious damage. You are a bright girl, and you can go far. That's why I spent money on all those extra classes."

"And it paid off. I got accepted in all the universities I applied for," Jewel said smugly, sitting up in the bed and rubbing her eyes.

Pearl sat at the end of the bed and sighed. "I've been wracking my brain to find out how to send you to college. I came up with two options. First, I considered your good-for-nothing father."

Jewel sighed. "And what did he say?"

Darnell Webb was the definition of a deadbeat. First, he had denied she was his before she was born. Then when she came out looking exactly like him and his family, he insisted on a DNA test because it could have been any of his brothers who fathered her.

Poor Pearl, she had the time of her life as a broke teenager on her own, while trying to get Darnell on child support. And when she was finally granted a reprieve by the court, Darnell was often in arrears. For most of her childhood years, her mother was dragging Darnell to court.

Her mother's life was a cautionary tale for any young girl, especially her. Jewel had been determined to not end up like her.

"Mom?" She prompted Pearl, who was looking out into space, a snarl on her lips. "What did Darnell say?"

"He said you should work first and then pay for college; thousands of people do it every day."

"That sounds like the standard Darnell reply," Jewel said. "I expected it, to be honest. Didn't he just get another child with his girlfriend? He doesn't have money to spare."

"He has four taxis on the road," Pearl scoffed. "He can afford to at least contribute to your college funds. I had to threaten him to take him to court to get every spare cent he contributed to your welfare outside of what the court ordered him to pay. He could redeem himself and at least help you with college."

Jewel sighed. It could take all morning when her mother started going off about Darnell. "What's the second option?" Jewel asked, trying to speed up the conversation and avoiding the vitriol that would follow.

"Your uncle Leonard," Pearl said, looking down at her hands.

"No," Jewel said. "Oh no. Not him. Never him."

"I already ran it by him, and he said he would pay for your college, pay for your lodgment in Kingston, give you pocket money and give you one of his cars that he is not using…."

"In exchange for what?" Jewel whispered. She knew the answer; there were no freebies from Leonard Crooks, her so-called uncle, her mother's benefactor.

"You pay him back," Pearl laid on the bed and stared at the ceiling. "Because you are family, he'll give you two years after college to pay it back."

"Two years?" Jewel sighed, "I'll have to get a well-paying job."

"Or you can marry a rich man." Pearl turned and looked at her. "You are a pretty girl. If it's one thing your lousy sperm donor of a father has given you is the Webb genes. Use them."

"Why is there always something with this family?" Jewel mumbled, "you can't get a break."

"If you don't pay Leonard back in cash, you will have to pay him back in kind," Pearl said. "You know how it is with your uncle."

"He is sick," Jewel said. "And stop calling him my uncle."

"He is my stepbrother," Pearl grimaced, "and he is why we are not living on the streets, and I have a job. He built us this lovely little place on family land and allows me to run Sensuous City. Without him, where would you and I be?"

"For years you had to pay for it on your back," Jewel said. "He wouldn't even allow you to have a proper relationship with anyone because he is always in the background watching and controlling you. I don't want the same deal. I want to go to college but not that badly. I will work for a while and then take out student loans."

"Or you can go to college, work hard, and get a scholarship." Pearl turned to her. "If Leonard only pays for a year or two, you can pay him back quickly after two years."

Jewel nodded. "That sounds better."

"And be picky about the boys that buzz around you," Pearl

said seriously. "Only pay attention to the rich ones. The ones that can afford to step in when you need it. And not just any ordinary rich boy either; target one from a rich family. And don't, for God's sake, have sex with anyone unless there is a ring involved. There is to be no free milk. They are going to have to buy the cow."

Jewel snickered. "You are a fine one to talk."

"I am the best person to tell you this," Pearl said. "I see so many girls and women come to Sensuous City. They all have the same story, with a little variation. They all slept with some man who discarded them after a while. They either have a kid or two or three for these men who disappear as soon as they get what they want. They didn't learn to think highly of themselves. You are not them. You are my precious Jewel, and you will do better than I did in relationships and better than any woman in our family so far."

Jewel was nodding vigorously. She was all for that. There was not one successful relationship in her family. At least none that she knew about, the couples may stay together, but they were as toxic as can be. "Where does love come into this?"

"Love is good but not necessary." Pearl scoffed. "Love is for people in romance novels or fairy tales. This is the real-world, Jewel; you have to approach relationships like a business. You are young and beautiful, don't waste your good years on a man that isn't worth it. If you are smart about this, then you will go far, mark my words."

Discover Exclusive Offers and Be the First to Know!

If you haven't already, don't miss out on the opportunity to join my New Release Newsletter! Sign up today and become part of an exclusive community where you'll be among the first to hear about my latest book releases and take advantage of special prices.

Why join my mailing list?

Be the First: Get a head start and be the first to know when I release a new book.

Exclusive Discounts: Unlock special prices available only to subscribers. Enjoy limited time offers and save big on your favorite books.

Quick and Easy: Signing up takes less than 30 seconds.

To join, visit https://www.brenalbar.com/newsletter or scan the QR code below.

Thank you for your support, and happy reading!

The Crimson Hill Series

Where family drama, romance, and a touch of sci-fi blend seamlessly in the enchanting backdrop of a small town in Jamaica. Prepare to embark on an unforgettable journey as secrets unravel, passions ignite, and destinies intertwine.

No Goodbye (Book 1)
No Misunderstanding (Book 2)
No Ordinary Love (Book 3)
No Fairy Tale (Book 4)
No Letting Go (Book 5)
No Strings Attached (Book 6)
No More Mrs. Nice Girl (Book 7)
No Place Like You (Book 8)
Knight and Day (Book 8.5)
No Expectations (Book 9)
Ice and Fyre (Book 9.5)
No Surrender (Book 10)
No Time for Love (Book 11)
No Promises (Book 12)
Winter's Eve (Book 13)

The Wiley Brothers

Step into the world of the Wiley Brothers, where tragedy weaves an unbreakable bond and love becomes their guiding light. In this captivating series, follow the journey of six remarkable boys as they navigate the tumultuous path of growing up without parents, discovering love, and finding their place in a challenging world.

Between Brothers (Book 0)- How it all began…
For Pete's Sake (Book 1)- Preston's story.
Crossing Jordan (Book 2)-Jordan's story.
Fire and Walter (Book 3)- Walter's story.
The Perfect Guy (Book 4)-Guy's Story.
The Patience of a Saint (Book 5)- Saint's Story.
A Case of Love (Book 6)- Case's Story.

The Pryce Sisters

Follow the remarkable journey of the Pryce triplets as they navigate the complexities of growing up, discovering romance, and embracing the exhilarating challenges of the new adult years.

Baby For A Pryce- Book 1
Right Pryce Wrong Time – Book 2
Yours, For A Pryce- Book 3

The Jacksons

Prepare to be enthralled by the captivating saga of the Jackson family. In this gripping series, secrets unravel, paternity questions loom, and love blooms in the most unexpected corners.

Ace- Book 1
Deuce- Book 2
Trey- Book 3
Quade- Book 4

The Scarlett Series

Their patriarch died and unexpectedly left each of them a fortune. Watch as the Scarlett family navigate their way through the ups and downs of sudden wealth, family secrets, and the complicated dynamics of their relationships.

Scarlett Baby (Book 1)
Scarlett Sinner (Book 2)
Scarlett Secret (Book 3)
Scarlett Love (Book 4)
Scarlett Promise (Book 5)
Scarlett Bride (Book 6)
Scarlett Heart (Book 7)

Magnolia Sisters

They were the rejects. The worst of the lot, they grew up in a girl's home together and formed sisterly bonds. Each book in the series tells the story of a different girl and the unique struggles and triumphs she faces along the way. With themes of friendship, forgiveness, and the power of love, the "Magnolia Sisters" series is a heartwarming and inspiring read that you won't want to put down.

Dear Mystery Guy- Book 1
Bad Girl Blues- Book 2
Her Mistaken Dream- Book 3
Just Like Yesterday – Book 4

New Song Series

A group of friends started out as a church band, see how each of them navigate their personal and professional lives while staying true to their faith and facing challenges along the way. With themes of forgiveness, redemption, and second chances, the New Song Series is a captivating read for anyone who enjoys heartwarming stories of love and faith.

Going Solo- Book 1
Duet on Fire- Book 2
Tangled Chords- Book 3
Broken Harmony- Book 4
A Past Refrain- Book 5
Perfect Melody- Book 6

The Bancrofts

The Bancroft family delves into the inner workings of academia and the high-stakes world of university politics. The family wrestles with the pressures of maintaining their family's legacy, they must confront their own demons and navigate the complex relationships that bind them together. From unexpected love affairs and betrayals to scandals and secrets that threaten to tear them apart, this is a series that will keep you captivated until the very end.

Homely Girl- Book 0
Saving Face- Book 1
Tattered Tiara- Book 2
Private Dancer- Book 3
Goodbye Lonely- Book 4
Practice Run- Book 5
Sense of Rumor- Book 6
A Younger Man- Book 7
Just To See Her- Book 8

Three Rivers Series

Three Rivers Series, a captivating tale of love, redemption, and second chances set in a picturesque community in St. Ann's Bay, Jamaica.

Private Sins- Book 1
Loving Mr. Wright- Book 2
Unholy Matrimony- Book 3
If It Ain't Broke- Book 4

The Resetter Series

The Resetter Series takes a look at a rare kind of person, a person who can travel back in time, but they only have one chance to get things right if they go back! With themes of second chances, changing the past and the power of love, the resetters series is a captivating time travel romance that many readers have described as a page turner.

Never Too Late- Book 1
Never Say Never- Book 2
Now or Never- Book 3
Almost Never- Book 4

On the Rebound Series

Experience the gripping and emotionally charged On the Rebound series, where love, betrayal, and redemption collide in a whirlwind of passion and secrets. Brace yourself for a journey filled with drama, cheating scandals, DNA questions, and ultimately, the power of second chances and finding love again.

On the Rebound- Book 1
On the Rebound Book 2

Standalone Books

Full Circle- After graduating from university, Diana wanted to return to Jamaica to find her siblings. What she didn't foresee was that she would meet Robert Cassidy and that both their pasts would be intertwined, and that disturbing questions would pop up about their parentage just when they were getting close.

After the End- Torn between two lovers. Colleen married her high school sweetheart, Isaiah, hoping that they would live happily ever after, but life intruded, and Isaiah disappeared at sea. She found work with the rich and handsome Enrique Lopez as a housekeeper and realized that she couldn't keep him at arm's length.

Love Triangle: Three Sides to the Story- George, the husband. Marie, the wife, and Karen-the mistress. They all get to tell their side of the story.

New Beginnings- Inner-city girl Geneva was offered an opportunity of a lifetime when she learned that her 'real' father was a wealthy man. Her decision to live up-town meant she had to leave Froggie, her 'ghetto don,' behind. She also found herself battling with her stepmother and battling her emotions for Justin, a suave up-towner.

The Preacher and the Prostitute- Prostitution and the clergy don't mix. Tell that to ex-prostitute Maribel, who finds herself in love with the Pastor at her church. Can an ex-prostitute and a pastor have a future together?

Historical Fiction

You won't want to miss out on these two captivating reads!

"The Pull of Freedom" tells the story of a slave family and their desperate struggle for freedom in Jamaica's colonial era. Follow the journey of these brave individuals as they fight for their right to be free, facing danger, heartbreak, and unimaginable obstacles along the way.

"The Empty Hammock" takes readers on a journey through time, as a modern woman finds herself transported back to the Taino era of Jamaica's history. Experience the wonder and mystery of this ancient culture through her eyes, as she learns about their traditions, beliefs, and way of life. With richly drawn characters and a beautifully realized setting, "The Empty Hammock" is a must-read for anyone who loves historical fiction that transports them to another time and place.

Short Story Collections

Di Taxi Ride and Other Stories- Funny stories about Jamaican life to make you laugh.

Book Bundles

Jamaican Romance Bundle- New Beginnings, Full Circle, Love Triangle: Three Sides to The Story, After The End

Wiley Brothers Book 0-3
Wiley Brothers Book 4-6